INTERSTELLAR ROAMING

Interstellar Roaming is a work of fiction. Names, characters, places, and incidents are the products of the author's imagination or are used fictitiously. Any resemblance to actual events, locales, or persons, living or dead, is entirely coincidental.

Published in the United States by IngramSpark

INTERSTELLAR ROAMING

YANK SHI

Contents

Foreword

The Divine Artifact

n the novel *World's End and the Sea Angle*, David and Emily were graduate students at the University of Colorado at Boulder, Colorado, USA. They met and fell in love on *campus*, and they often chatted and discussed Heaven and the Earth after classes. Common interests and ideals brought them together.

In the year 2010, when David was flying a hot air balloon, he was taken by a strong tornado to a space-time tunnel that traversed backward, and went through alone to the East African prairie one million years ago. That was the prehistoric age of mankind. He lived with the primitive people there for nearly a year, experiencing fantasy and adventure. Later, he returned to the United States through a space-time tunnel.

In 2012, David and Emily accidentally encountered strong winds and waves during a Bermuda expedition. Their small plane was destroyed, and the two of them fell into the whirlpool in the sea. Unexpectedly, they were brought into a space-time tunnel leading to the future. Both of them came to Australia a thousand years later. At that time, human society was rational and peaceful. There was no money, no government, no army, and science and technology were highly developed. Society was almost perfect. However, David and Emily had the misfortune of encountering the world's end and were nearly destroyed together with the doom of the world. David and Emily did not belong to the future world. That's why a mysterious force fantastically sent them back to the sea off southeastern Florida through a reverse space-time tunnel—the very origin of their journey. They returned from Florida to Boulder, Colorado, to reunite with their relatives and friends there.

In 2019, they unexpectedly welcomed their daughter, Sophia, who had lost contact with them for four years. Sophia was born in the future world and was already 7 years old. David's parents had taken care of their grandson, Oliver, for many years, and now a lovely girl Sophia came down from the sky. David's parents loved these children so much that they were willing to live together with David's family.

After David's father retired, he gave his spacious office to David and Emily, who usually dealt with data sorting and scientific research here.

In the speculative and fantastical sequel of the novel *World's End and the Sea Angle*, in the final chapter of the sequel "*The Sword of Damocles,*" David and Emily experience a 'possible nuclear war.' Among the violent nuclear explosions, they embrace tightly with infinite love.

While David hums a lyric tune and Emily's eyes shine with tears of happiness, they calmly end their short but colorful lives. However, when the current story takes place, the 'possible nuclear war' has not yet occurred, and the sword of Damocles has not yet fallen upon humanity. Therefore, David and Emily are still alive.

They are still full of vigor and are going to write a new chapter with the rest of their lives, acting out the following scenario in the current book.

Through their personal experiences and painstaking study across time and space, David and Emily greatly expanded their knowledge, broadened their minds, and sharpened their vision, making it deeper and farther-reaching. With their foresight and extraordinary spirituality, David and Emily recognized the root of all things in the world and realized the greatness and omnipotence of God.

They had begun deciphering the mysteries of the origination and extinction of all things in the world, as well as the layered governance and orderly intertwining of the planets. They realized the profound truth of 'the unity of spirit and matter' and 'the creation by Heaven and Earth,' and proposed the reasoning that 'materialism' and 'idealism' are mutually inclusive, and 'evolution' and 'creation' go hand in hand David and Emily's superb insights and philosophical theories were deeply appreciated by Heaven.

God believed that David and Emily were the rare people who could control this opportunity and crux.

In addition, David and Emily had repeatedly done good and righteous deeds for the people, thus achieving their perfect personalities. They received the love of God.

David and Emily each had a strange dream on the same night. They were granted an "artifact" in their dreams. That was a *Divine Watch with a Magic Spell.*

God gave each of them a face-to-face advice in their dreams.

This Divine Watch was directly attached to the pocket watch that David usually carried with him. David made adjustments to the knob of the watch. By pulling out the knob a little, the Divine Watch would be turned on. Once turned on, the owner of this Divine Watch could see numerous options at different coordinates in his mind. The image that appeared in David's mind at this time seemed to be a computer screen, and various options were vividly visible. When David stopped adjusting the knob and pushed it down in a click, the planned position on the coordinates was determined.

The space-time coordinates of travel destinations were almost unlimited. In terms of distance, it could cruise freely near or far, in a small local area, or beyond a very large area without a limit. Its ability was far beyond reaching other planets in spaceships, and also beyond the 'miracle' of traveling through space-time tunnels. However, this Divine Watch could only determine the location of the destination.

The starting mechanism of the voyage also required a magical command. God granted Emily the power, which was a Magic Spell. This Magic Spell was issued in a mysterious language, which was unknown to the public, but only existed in the mind of the holder of the Magic Spell. Emily could express her intention by voice input, which was equivalent to a start command. In other words, the Divine Watch and Magic Spell could only unleash their power when both holders worked together, thereby achieving the holders' purpose. The Divine Watch and Magic Spell connected David and Emily together, and the magic power could only be exercised on them, not others.

In the dreams of David and Emily, God told them that this artifact had boundless power. It could help them achieve some goals that were initially impossible to achieve and also helped them escape from danger and difficulties. The most important thing was that this artifact could help them gain experience, broaden their horizons, open minds for all of humanity, and rid them of ignorance. God hoped that they would live up to His high trust and shoulder this heavy responsibility. At the same time, they must work together to effectively use this artifact.

When David and Emily woke up from their dreams, they agreed to experiment to determine whether the artifact obtained in their dreams was effective.

David: Go ahead, Emily, give me a goal to move forward.

Emily: We'll be in the city of Portland right away.

David: OK, no problem. I've been confirmed to go Portland on the Divine Watch.

Emily: To Portland, Oregon, not Portland, Maine.

David: Of course, I have designated Portland, Oregon. Otherwise, it will be 'a slight error, a thousand miles away.' Don't worry, I will not be mistaken.

Emily: If it is a cosmic leap, the error caused by a single mistake will be more than a thousand miles!

David: All right, all right. I have fixed the position. It's Portland, Oregon. Emily, please give me your order.

Emily: OK.

Emily silently recited the Magic Spell she learned in her dream last night. In an instant, the environment in front of them changed to the streets of Portland.

The streets were full of traffic; the roadsides were lined with green trees. The humid and mild climate was suitable for the growth of all kinds of plants. Almost every courtyard had Japanese maple trees with red leaves.

After all, Colorado was different. The state was located on the plateau, where many trees could not grow. There were many conifers such as pine and cypress, the scene was completely different from Oregon.

David and Emily were stunned and puzzled; it was so incredible. They were no strangers to Portland, having visited several times for sightseeing. What baffled them was how they had ended up here from Boulder—over twelve hundred miles away. They hadn't driven, nor had they taken a flight, yet they had arrived so quickly that the journey felt as if it had never happened at all. No matter how advanced the spacecraft or how fast space travel became, it still required time. Yet, when they returned to Boulder, Colorado, it happened in an instant—bringing them back almost to the spot where they had started.

The miraculous and boundless power of this Divine Watch and the Magic Spell could make the two people freely change their time and space coordinates in space, even from one planet to another planet, from one galaxy to another galaxy, and from one universe to another universe without having to go through the usual space-time tunnel. David and Emily thus took a shortcut through time. Using this Divine Watch, they could choose any location they wanted to go to in the vast space. Once using this Magic Spell, they could reach their destination in an instant, get rid of any predicament, and turn danger into a breeze.

The time and space travel experienced by David and Emily before was a passive time travel by entering a small-scale time and space tunnel inadvertently.

But now that they had a universal artifact, they could choose targets to travel in a wider range, beyond the solar system, and even beyond the universe they currently lived in, to carry out abnormal fantasy travel. The time taken for this kind of crossing was infinitely shortened, even negligible. Only God's artifact could help them achieve this miracle.

David and Emily originally loved tourism and exploration and were keen on exploring the sky, the Earth, and the people. It should be said that they were philosophical explorers.

As they wished today, they would personally experience a brand-new, vast, and colorful world.

If their journey was meant to be extraordinary, then it would be unlike any other—a voyage of pure will, where travelers chose their destination and arrived instantly, without the burden of time.

Now, they had such a universal treasure. It could help them achieve various goals that were almost unimaginable in the past and enable them to travel around or beyond the world. David and Emily were so excited that they hugged each other and sang heartily.

David: With this artifact, we can go to more distant planets and more places to explore the mysteries of the universe.

Emily: With the help of God, we can gallop across the universe and see more anecdotes.

David: It would be a great pity if we didn't travel and put our artifact on the shelf.

Emily: That's like keeping one's *thousand-mile horse* in a pen all day long, making it useless.

David: It is already 8 years since we went to Bermuda and traveled to the future.

Emily: We were in high spirits back then. Do you still have the courage you used to have?

David: I don't think I've lost my courage. How about you, Emily?

Emily: Me? It's hard to say. Isn't it insane for one to leave one's home and run so far in one's middle age?

David: If you don't go, the artifact can only be discarded. The artifact must be used with the cooperation of the two of us. If you don't go, I can't go either.

Emily: David, do you believe what I just said?

David: Were you kidding me?

Emily: You know me best. I also know you best. Both of us are "restless" people. I can't wait. You have to start now, I'm afraid you can't wait, either.

David: Just like you, I can't wait. Then let's set off on an expedition day.

Emily: It's a deal.

David: Deal.

David and Emily found that this Divine Watch was especially miraculous. In addition to the positioning function, it also had some other functions that needed to be explored during use.

For example, by adjusting the figure parameter of the Divine Watch holders, their height and weight could be changed.

David and Emily had a female cat Lily and a male dog Tommy. Lily and Tommy were loved by them.

That day, Lily was sleeping on the sofa, and Tommy was resting on the floor.

Emily suddenly had a whim and wanted to experiment with the function of using the Divine Watch to change their own figures.

Emily: David, let's become as big as Lily and Tommy. We should have about the same height as them and not be condescending. Let's experience that feeling, OK?

David: Sure. In that way, our relationship with Lily and Tommy will no longer be masters and pets, but friends and partners. See how they react.

Emily: Please set us to the size of dogs and cats on the Divine Watch.

David: OK.

Emily silently recited the Magic Spell. After a while, David and Emily shrunk at the same time and finally reduced to the level close to dogs and cats. Lily and Tommy looked at their masters in amazement and blinked inexplicably. They came forward and licked their master's face as usual. They were still so affectionate and friendly, but the distance between them was greatly reduced.

Strangely, when the bodies of David and Emily shrank, their clothes also shrank. This was because human clothes were somewhat like animal fur. Fur was inseparable from the body.

Their Divine Watch was even more amazing than they initially imagined. It would become bigger and smaller as the holder's body expanded and contracted.

At this time, Lily seemed to suddenly grow a lot bigger in their eyes. She was like a tiger. The mischievous tiger squatted there motionless, gathered all her strength, and then swooped at Emily. Emily was thrown down, laughing and wrestling with the tiger.

The dog Tommy looked much larger than before, simply like a hippopotamus. It came over and bit David's belt, lifted David up, and tossed him around. David yelled at him, "Tommy, stop it, stop it!" Tommy obediently put David down.

David and Emily lay on the carpet, laughing.

At this moment, Sophia hurriedly opened the door and walked into the office to look for Lily.

Sophia screamed in horror at the sight of her parents—shrunken to unnaturally tiny figures, as if she had stumbled upon monsters in the glaring light of day. In a panic, she hurried out of the room.

She told her grandpa, grandma, and her brother about the strange thing. Nobody could believe their ears, wondering if Sophia had mistaken it. There could not be such things in the world.

The four of them walked into David and Emily's office together, but they didn't see the miracle Sophia described. David and Emily were the same as before, their figures had not been changed.

David and Emily had miraculously returned to their original figures after

Sophia left. Sophia insisted that she had said correctly just now. She said that her parents were as big as Lily, lying on the carpet, not as tall as Tommy.

After repeated questioning by everyone, David and Emily told the truth.

David and Emily said that God had given them a Divine Watch with a Magic Spell. This artifact had boundless power. They could use this artifact to go to any other planet in the universe, or even to any planet in the parallel universe outside their universe. By adjusting the chronological coordinate, they could also go to any past or future era, like their previous time journeys. In addition, their height and volume could also be adjusted to the required scale, expand, or shrink. The situation that Sophia just saw was not absurd, it was achieved with the help of that artifact.

Sophia: Just now, I saw my parents became so small. I was scared. I don't want to see you changing back and forth like that again. It's horrible.

At this time, David went to the bathroom.

David's mother held Emily's hands and stared at her eyes, as if to say, *Good daughter-in-law, don't go out so far again!*

When David returned to the office, his father asked him directly.

David's father: Now that you have this artifact, are you going to travel again?

David: Yes, we used to travel passively in the space-time dimensions of the Earth. This time, it's different. The span will be far beyond the Earth. And everything is under our control.

David's father: Both of you are about forty years old, and the children are still young. It's better to stay at home, take care of yourselves and your children, and enjoy the family's happiness. It's okay to do some research at home.

David's mother: Children, this kind of travel is too dangerous. The previous two journeys made everyone worried about you. We thought you were dead and set up a tombstone for you in the cemetery. We are so old, and your two children also need to be cared for and accompanied. So please give us some peace.

David: Mom and Dad, you are right. We really can't bear to leave our relatives again. But this time, we are blessed and entrusted by God. We really want to use the rest of our lives to do something for human beings and to dedicate the remaining heat of our lives to the world.

Emily: You don't have to worry about it, we have this artifact this time, so we can avoid danger and disaster when we are outside. It's easy for us to come back when we want to. As long as we adjust our watch and read the spell, we can return to your side immediately.

At this time, David suddenly found that his amulet was missing. Searching around indoors, nowhere to be seen.

Emily: David, did you leave your watch beside the washbasin when you went to the bathroom just now?

David: Right, right. I did look at the time on the watch and set it aside.

David went to the bathroom to look for it, but he didn't find it.

David: That's bad. We can't do anything without the watch.

Emily: Well, I can recite the Magic Spell. Remember that when I recited the Magic Spell, the Divine Watch would vibrate. Let's search inside and outside carefully to see if we can find it.

Emily began to chant a spell, and David was looking for the watch. David asked their dog Tommy to look for it. Later, Tommy barked at the pond in the backyard. David saw small ripples on the water surface of the pond. He thought it was probably caused by the trembling of the Divine Watch in the water, and asked Tommy to fish it out of the water. Tommy dived into the water, took out the watch with his mouth, and handed it to David. David checked the Divine Watch carefully and found that the watch hadn't lost its function due to water immersion.

David: Thank you, Tommy.

David wondered how the watch fell into the pool.

David: Who did it?

Emily: Lily, did you do it? Lily shook her head in denial.

At this time, Sophia stood up and took responsibility

Sophia: Dad, Mom, you don't have to ask. I was the one who threw the damn thing into the water. I don't want to see my Dad and Mom become so small, nor do I want you to leave home and go so far away. I traveled alone from the Wonderland and stayed in an orphanage for several years. I just reunited with you, and you have to leave again. It's all because of that damncd watch that you're leaving, I hate that thing.

David: Good girl, I understand how you feel.

Oliver: I think it's a once-in-a-lifetime opportunity for Mom and Dad to have this artifact. You should go to the outside world, Mom and Dad, I also want to go with you.

David: We also want to take you with us, my son. But the magic power of that artifact is only effective to me and your mother.

Emily: Son, wait for a chance later. You need to complete your studies now. Stay at home and accompany your elderly grandparents and younger sister at home when we are away.

Oliver: I see.

Sophia: I still hope that our parents will stay. We used to gather less and leave more. The whole family is finally reunited, and you have to leave again.

Emily: Actually, we would like to stay at home with you. Ok, let's give up this opportunity and stop traveling, OK?

Sophia came forward and hugged Mom and Dad.

Sophia: Great! Good father, good mother!

So, David and Emily did not go as planned.

David and Emily realized that their future travels would greatly exceed their previous travels in terms of time and space. The distance would be farther and the time longer. They had already reached the middle age. They couldn't take the children out to adventure, nor did they want to delay their studies.

2020 AD

One morning, David's parents discovered that David and Emily had disappeared without a trace, without saying goodbye to anyone in the family.

David's parents had guessed something.

They found a letter left by David and Emily to their parents and children on David's desk.

They said in their letter:

Dear parents, lovely son Oliver,
and daughter Sophia,

we love each of you. Please forgive us for leaving without saying goodbye to you. Please forgive us for our willful behavior this time. At a time when we are middle-aged, this trip is indeed an unprecedented one. We are going to some planets in another universe to explore. As the saying goes, "When parents are alive, do not travel far away." We are well aware that this journey defied that traditional wisdom.

However, this time, we are definitely not going sightseeing and entertainment. Instead, we want to do some research and exploration about human beings, the world, and the universe. The data collected from planets beyond the known universe will be analyzed and compared with data from the universe and Earth, allowing for more accurate conclusions.

We want to dedicate the results of our investigations to the world and mankind today and make our own contributions in our lifetime. The Almighty God gave us the magic artifact, and we are grateful for it.

We are willing to complete the sacred mission entrusted to us by God with our modest strength. We will strive to do a good job in this investigation.

Goodbye, parents and children. We know that the journey is bound to be full of risks. It is also possible that we will never come back again. In that case, *we bid farewell forever to you at this moment. We sincerely thank our parents for your upbringing and teaching. Dear parents, after we leave home, the care of the children will be entrusted to you. We cannot thank you enough for it.*

Oliver and Sophia, you should live well, study hard, keep forging ahead, and have a promising future. We wish you all happiness and health.

Suppose, we do not come back if something goes wrong, please find a place for us in the cemetery, erect a tombstone, and link our names together. We were born on Earth, and our souls will return to Earth, to our homeland. Thanks.

We have the blessing and protection of God, and the help of the artifact. We believe that everything will be as expected and look forward to our reunion in the future.

David Polo and Emily Polo

In this way, David and Emily left home again. Relatives were blessing them.

Chapter 1

THE DINOSAUR WORLD

For David and Emily, this was their first expedition with the help of their Divine Watch and Magic Spell. After many discussions before their departure, the two of them compared various options given on the Divine Watch. First of all, they decided to explore stars in another parallel universe, which was something that modern space scientists and astronauts dared not to imagine. Even with the help of a space-time tunnel, it was very unlikely to reach another universe outside our universe. This goal seemed quite tempting to David and Emily. They named the unknown universe Universe B. The universe where they were now was naturally Universe A.

Because today's astronomers can only name the galaxies and stars in our universe, the names of galaxies and stars in other universes could only "be wanting" at present.

Like Universe A, Universe B contained countless galaxies of varying sizes.

David and Emily extracted a large galaxy from Universe B and named it Silver

Way, which corresponded to the Milky Way of Universe A. In the Silver Way Galaxy, there was also a "Big Sun system" corresponding to the Solar system in the Milky Way. There were nearly one hundred planets in this Big Sun system, which was much larger than the Solar system.

In the Silver Way system of Universe B, most of the stars were barren places where natural conditions were not suitable for biological survival, or the temperature there was either too low or too high, there was a lack of water or air, or the ultraviolet intensity was not suitable for biological survival, etc.

The planet extracted by David and Emily must be inhabited by advanced organisms and humans, or there was the possibility for advanced organisms and even humans to live on it. Otherwise, the investigation would be meaningless.

In determining the time coordinate, David had some whims this time.

David: Emily, the last time I traveled by myself to the prehistoric hominids of East Africa was a million years ago. This time, I want to go to a planet hundreds of millions of years ago, where there may be large creatures like dinosaurs.

Emily: David, aren't you afraid of them?

David: You know, I like dinosaurs since childhood. I like to watch cartoons and horror films with dinosaurs. It would be so much fun and fascinating if we saw real dinosaurs!

Emily: All right. Just do as you like. Anyway, we have the Divine Watch given by God, and when we encounter difficulties, we can ask the Divine Watch to help us out of the predicament.

David: Yes. I'll take a look. The Divine Watch shows that there is a planet in the Big Sun system in the Silver Way, which is somewhat similar to our Earth. We can call it Dasor. There are natural environments and resources for human survival. Before humans appeared, the planet was dominated by large animals like dinosaurs. In my opinion, this is exactly my dream place.

Emily: David, please set the target at Dasor in the Silver Way system of Universe B. The time coordinate is set at minus 200 million years, that is, 200 million years ago. When everything is ready, I will use the Magic Spell to activate the target on the Divine Watch.

David: Everything is ready. I left the letter to our family on my desk.

Emily: I also brought several packets of compressed biscuits and 2 bottles of water, just in case.

David: Great! Let's go, Emily.

How magical and fascinating it was to travel and explore the wild world hundreds of millions of years ago! This was a pioneering work that ordinary people dared not think about, and it was also something that human beings could not do now. Even if there was a space-time tunnel leading to hundreds of millions of years ago, it would be far away and time-consuming.

David and Emily could easily achieve their goals with their Divine Watch and Magic Spell now.

Emily muttered a spell silently.

David and Emily disappeared from their home office.

In a blink of an eye, they found themselves in a strange wilderness. The temperature here was slightly higher, and the flowers, plants, and trees were extremely luxuriant. Weeds had broad leaves and long stems, resembling both ferns and plantains. Looking around, the species of plants were almost completely different from those on Earth.

This was much more magical than the trip last time when they crossed from Bermuda to Wonderland. It was just like a magician's magic performance. The miraculous power and instant conversion made them dizzy and amazed. David and Emily were watching the surrounding environment excitedly and comparing it with the Earth's.

David: It looks more primitive and weird than East Africa a million years ago.

Emily: And everything here is so natural. I like the environment and the original ecology.

David and Emily looked for something to eat in this strange wasteland. Soon, they picked some wild fruits and berries, which were rich in taste and sweet in juice. The two also drank some water from the clear stream. David and Emily arrived here in the local afternoon. Soon, the night fell.

That night. They found that the sky here was particularly clean, and so was the atmosphere. The sky was full of bright stars.

David and Emily discovered that the sky here was filled with countless more stars than they had ever seen with the naked eye on Earth. They looked at the sky, as if through an astronomical telescope, they saw clusters of nebulae. Those were some galaxies. Because they were in a different universe, they had noticed that the distribution of stars in the sky here was completely different from what they saw on Earth. It was a completely strange star map. No Polaris, when t Uranus, etc., could be seen. Besides, there was no moon around the planet in the sky, it was a moonless sky. The entire sky was changed, and they realized that they were in a completely new environment.

David and Emily lay in the grass of primitive plants and fell asleep all night. When they woke up, the sky was gradually brightened. A bright star like the sun was rising from the sea level in the distance. It seemed somewhat like on the Earth, and somewhat didn't. This planet was bigger and brighter than the sun of the solar system. They called this bright planet the Big Sun.

At the same time, David and Emily heard some strange calls, some like birds and some like animals.

David and Emily began to notice traces of animals in the distance. Those were some animals that they had never seen before.

Most of them were enormous, appearing even larger as these creatures drew near. David and Emily, for lack of a better term, called them "dinosaurs," as they resembled the extinct creatures from Earth.

The dinosaurs seemed to have discovered that some strange animals appeared in their territory. They came over one after another to see what was going on.

When David and Emily first saw these giants and didn't know their hearts, it was inevitable that they felt a bit awkward and embarrassed.

However, David and Emily were not afraid of them and even greeted them with gestures. With their long necks stretched out, these giant beasts looked curiously at them, like a group of turkeys, who saw two strange little birds on the ground.

One of these beasts extended his mouth and nostrils to David's face. David gently touched it with his hand and made a friendly gesture. Not wanting to experience this stimulation, the dinosaur tightened his throat and sneezed loudly. Fortunately, the dinosaur turned his head and sneezed to the side. If the sneeze struck David head-on, it would be a storm too fierce to withstand.

These dinosaurs carefully observed the two small animals in front of them, and saw that they were not hostile or malicious; they were friendly to them, so they did not hurt them.

Furthermore, these dinosaurs were herbivorous. Had they encountered carnivorous dinosaurs, the fate of the two guests might have been different.

This was really a world of dinosaurs. There were flying dinosaurs in the sky, reptile dinosaurs walking on land, and swimming dinosaurs swimming in the water. David and Emily set up a shelter under a big tree, where they rested and slept, and were ready to live there for some time.

What surprised David and Emily most was that since they came to the star Dasor in the Silver Way of Universe B, they found that they seemed to be much younger, about

20 years younger than they were on Earth. David seemed to become a young man, and Emily became a young girl.

They were more energetic; had endless energy and never felt tired. David and Emily noticed that the day and night here were much longer than the day and night on the Earth, nearly twice as long as the Earth's day and night. There was no moon here, so there was no concept of "month." A year here was naturally longer than a year on Earth, almost twice the Earth year. According to the chronology here, the ages of David and Emily had also shrunk by half.

Although ages of different chronologies should not affect the degree of biological aging, yet for David and Emily—the aliens from another universe—it could actually have the effect of rejuvenation. This might be due to the differences in the time dimension of different universes and the prompt changes in the environment.

Later, David and Emily discovered on the Divine Watch that the Silver Way Galaxy where they were now was much larger than the Milky Way, and the Big Sun system here was also several times larger than the solar system.

Since then, David and Emily lived with the giant animals there and developed friendships with them.

David and Emily discovered that as long as people were friendly to animals and did not harm them, they would not harm humans, and in some cases, they would even form a deep and close relationship with humans. On Earth, there were those who formed close bonds with lions, and a woman who ventured into the wild forests of Africa to observe orangutans, living harmoniously with them. In China, another woman adopted a wolf cub from a young age, raising it as her own. When the wolf cub grew up, it became a good friend of the woman for many years. After returning to the wilderness, he still remembered their old love. Among the dinosaurs was a female whom David and Emily called

They had a close relationship with each other, caressing and helping each other. Amanda was familiar with everything there here and often helped David and Emily find good food.

Sometimes they got together to eat and tease each other.

Plus, the dinosaurs here belonged to one group.

Their leader was a gigantic male dinosaur. David and Emily called him Peter. Peter looked mighty, quite the bearing of a beast king. He was very friendly to David and Emily. At times, he would let David and Emily sit on his tail and swing them around for fun. He also asked David and Emily to climb up to his back along his tail, and he carried them on the ground. David and Emily were very comfortable on the back of the giant dinosaur, like riding an elephant on Earth.

David and Emily could find wild fruits and potatoes everywhere to satisfy their hunger. Occasionally, they also ate cooked food. They used the lighter brought by David to make a fire and cook something like wild grain, wild adverb potatoes, seafood like fish, shrimp, clams, etc. David had rich experience in this field. In their interactions with the dinosaurs, David and Emily exchanged greetings and information, gradually developing a vocal communication system—or a language— with them. Amanda, their best friend, was an integral part of this evolving connection. The throat of dinosaurs could emit a thick sound, expressing feelings and some kind of message, which was even like singing. Sometimes David and Emily also sang and danced with the dinosaurs. David and Emily found that these animals had a sense of music and rhythm, especially an expressive desire.

Dinosaurs weren't all friendly with each other. Once, a group of dinosaurs from other places invaded their territory. Those dinosaurs were carnivorous dinosaurs, and they were looking for food and drinking water here.

What was particularly hateful was that they liked to eat piles of dinosaur eggs on the ground. The dinosaurs here, led by the leader "Peter," launched a counterattack against the invaders. The two groups of giant beasts fought against each other.

David and Emily also joined the battle. Each of them held a wood branch to fight the enemy. A large enemy dinosaur bit the branch in Emily's hand, snatched it away, and threw it aside. Emily quickly dodged. The dinosaur opened his mouth and put Emily in it. David wanted to retrieve Emily from the dinosaur's mouth, but unexpectedly, the dinosaur held Emily up so that David could not reach her. At the most urgent moment, Peter, the leader, rushed to the enemy dinosaur, opened his mouth wide, and bit the neck of the enemy dinosaur with sharp teeth. The enemy dinosaur screamed, and Emily in his mouth fell to the ground. David rushed forward to pull Emily away. Fortunately, Emily was only slightly injured by the teeth of the dinosaur, and it was not serious.

Amanda also joined the battle. When she saw Emily being bitten by an enemy dinosaur, she rushed forward like crazy and fought the enemy to the death. During the fight, the enemy dinosaur stabbed Amanda's arm with his sharp horn, leaving a big wound on Amanda's shoulder.

After all, carnivorous dinosaurs were more fierce than herbivorous dinosaurs, and as invaders, carnivorous dinosaurs clearly had an advantage in this battle. Our dinosaur army, led by General Peter, fought bravely against the enemy, but suffered heavy casualties. Seeing this unfavorable situation, David and Emily had to appeal to their divine artifact. The two of them manipulated the artifact and suddenly grew taller, becoming two giants. The enemy dinosaurs were shocked and turned pale, as they were reduced to rats in front of the giants.

David and Emily crushed their arrogant enemies beneath their feet. One dinosaur tried to resist, sinking its teeth into David's ankle. With a swift movement, David raised his leg and violently kicked it aside, sending the creature flying into the air. It flipped through the sky several times before crashing to the ground. With a mournful cry, the dinosaur fell half-dead.

The other invading dinosaurs saw that their situation was not good, and immediately retreated, like scattering birds and beasts in confusion.

The invaders were defeated. The dinosaurs here had returned to normal life order.

The wound on Amanda's arm was still not healed. She endured the pain and supported her remaining dinosaur eggs. Because she was difficult to move, David and Emily helped her find food, like taking care of the wounded person. Amanda put her nose and mouth close to David and Emily's faces while wagging her tail to express her gratitude. David and Emily also found several broad leaves and grass stems to bandage Amanda's wounds to prevent mosquitoes and wild bees from biting them.

Amanda had a close friendship with David and Emily, they were not relatives but were better than relatives. Under the meticulous care of David and Emily, Amanda's wounds gradually healed. But a deep scar was left on Amanda's arm. It was a wound that formed a hole in the bone.

After a period of time, Amanda's eggs hatched several small dinosaurs. Amanda took good care of her baby dinosaurs with her natural maternal love. David and Emily also tried their best to help Amanda and get some food and drink for her children. Fortunately, food in the wild was not hard to find at that time, at least it was much more abundant than in the wilderness of the Earth.

Once, a group of flying dinosaurs landed in the wilderness as a temporary habitat. They were friendly with the herbivorous reptiles here, without conflict and mutual harm. They saw that David and Emily were a little different, and seemed to feel somewhat weird. David and Emily extended a friendly hand to them and offered them something to eat. They regarded the two as friends. Two of the larger flying dinosaurs let the two new friends climb on top of them, flew around the sky, and brought them back safely. David and Emily were flying through the sky on top of dinosaurs, and it was awesome. They seemed to be in a fairy tale world, roaming in the air. David had liked dinosaurs since he was a child, and now that his wish had come true, he was even more excited.

It was not known how long afterward, David noticed an important announcement on the Divine Watch that there would be a major disaster on the planet soon, and the creatures on the planet would be destroyed. Most of them would not survive. It was said that dinosaurs had roamed Earth for around 170 million years before vanishing after a small planet collided with Earth. The dinosaurs on this planet, Dasor, might one day share the same fate. Sure enough, after a few months, the originally mild climate here suddenly became cold, as if winter was approaching. Feeling bad, David and Emily discussed how to escape the planet. Although they were reluctant to leave their dinosaur friends here, they couldn't help them. This might be the arrangement of God, which was hard to disobey.

David and Emily decided to flee here, otherwise they would die in the coming disaster.

David and Emily endured the pain in their hearts and bid farewell to the dinosaur friends here one by one. The dinosaur friends knew that the two were going to leave and were also reluctant to part with them.

David and Emily set the destination of their trip in the human era hundreds of millions of years later in the time coordinate, and the space coordinate was set in the place where they were now. They wanted to see with their own eyes what everything here would look like hundreds of millions of years later.

When Emily gave an order, the two of them were in a completely different era in an instant, but they were still in the same place, exactly. It used to be a place where dinosaurs lived together, and it used to be a lush and luxuriant original ecology, but now it was a dry and cracked place without any vegetation, like a desolate area without human intervention.

David and Emily saw many dinosaur fossils on this wasteland. They realized that this was the place where they had just left. They felt as if they had just left here for a while. In fact, they had been gone for hundreds of millions of years. This surprised them greatly. Dinosaurs that were still alive and well just now had turned into fossils. What impressed David and Emily most was that they found the fossils of their friends Amanda and Peter in the bunch of dinosaur fossils. Peter was the tallest of the dinosaurs in the area at that time. It was easy to distinguish him from others. Amanda had a stab wound on her shoulder, which now formed a dent on the fossil. This wound was caused by the unfortunate injury of Amanda when she fought desperately with the enemy dinosaur to protect Emily. David and Emily knew for sure that this fossil was Amanda.

Emily hugged the fossil's leg, unwilling to let go for a long time. She kept shouting, "Amanda, Amanda!" Emily's eyes were filled with tears, and she choked up, sobbing uncontrollably. David's eyes were also wet. They came to Peter's fossil. The skeleton of that tall body had collapsed in hundreds of millions of years of vicissitudes. Parts of the body were found on the ground, forming scattered and miscellaneous fossils. David and Emily thought that this was the tall and mighty dinosaur leader "General Peter." David unconsciously took off his hat in salute to the battered fossil torso. Hundreds of millions of years of vicissitudes turned in a flash. How incredible, how touching!

There was another interesting story here. Before David and Emily left the dinosaur territory where they had lived, they found a dying baby dinosaur on the grass. He was so small and weak that he was deliberately abandoned by his parents. This kind of survival of the fittest was not uncommon in the animal kingdom.

Emily picked up the poor little dinosaur and fed him something to eat and drink. He actually survived. Although the adult dinosaurs were large, their eggs were usually small. This little dinosaur picked up was even smaller. David and Emily named him Bill.

Emily put Bill in her coat pocket. When they left the dinosaur territory, they decided to do an experiment. They would take this little dinosaur to the human era hundreds of millions of years later to see if he could survive. Even if they didn't take her away, he would surely die.

After the Divine Watch was activated, Emily tightly attached the little dinosaur to her body, almost becoming one with it. Even after David and Emily came to the world hundreds of millions of years later, this little dinosaur Bill, born hundreds of millions of years ago, actually survived. David and Emily were overjoyed. This was an unprecedented miracle!

David and Emily thought they had come to another era. However, they could no longer live on this wasteland. This place was no longer the environment with luxuriant foliage and wild fruits in the past. In order to survive, they must leave here and go to the city where humans live.

David showed the local map with the Divine Watch. On the map, they found that their current location was still quite a distance from the nearest city, Walon, and no roads or bus routes were going to it. However, the Divine Watch could help them. David adjusted the destination on the map displayed on the Watch, which was the nearby city of Walon. David and Emily reluctantly bid farewell to these dinosaur fossils and their former friends. They said they would visit them again in the future.

At Emily's command, they magically landed on an open land in the middle of the city of Walon.

When they walked around the street, they saw that the people here were larger in size than Earthlings, and their average height and weight were above the Earthlings. Whether this was caused by the Big Sun of the Big Sun system was still unknown.

David and Emily strike up a conversation with a passerby. Although the language was different, they could convey some meaning. The people here were rich in expression, warm, and friendly, and sometimes spoke with high and low intonation. Gradually, they understood each other's basic meaning.

David and Emily quickly adapted to life on Dasor, seamlessly integrating into the society of this era. They found work at a paleontological institute specializing in dinosaur research, yet their hearts often longed for the prehistoric age they had once experienced. They deeply missed the time of the dinosaurs—along with the friends they had left behind. As soon as they had leisure time, they would go to the distant wilderness to visit those old friends who had become fossils.

David and Emily had had a fruitful career in paleontological research. They had passed through the time and space tunnel of the Bermuda Triangle to the future world before they got the Divine Watch and Magic Spell. After returning from the future world, they gained a profound understanding of both the universe and their own existence. Reflecting on their experiences, they formulated the principles of *"the unity of spirit and matter"* and *"creation by Heaven and Earth."* After returning to the present world from the age of dinosaurs this time, they learned that the dinosaurs were not completely extinct. A small number of dinosaurs survived by adapting to the harsh environment, through their own adjustment and mutation. Some flying dinosaurs turned into birds. Some of the swimming dinosaurs turned into crocodiles, turtles, etc. This evolution had indeed changed species. It further proved the role of the objective environment in the "shaping" of organisms.

The Heaven could create things, and the Earth could set limits. Therefore, it was called *"created by Heaven and Earth."*

Creatures mutated due to changes in the objective environment, just as some wolves became dogs. Some wild animals had become livestock. David and Emily had thought that external force could not change the species and believed that dogs and wolves still belonged to the same species. Now it seemed that crocodiles, turtles, etc., evolved from dinosaurs and were not the same species as dinosaurs. Birds evolved from dinosaurs and did not belong to the same species as flying dinosaurs. The variation of some dinosaurs was obviously caused by *terrestrial design*. David and Emily did not believe that this kind of variation was the *evolution* of animals as described in the theory of evolution. It was difficult to say that geckos, crocodiles, turtles, and other creatures were more advanced than dinosaurs. The variation of organisms due to changes in the external environment was not *evolution*.

Changing species by external forces did not support the evolution of organisms from lower to higher levels.

After living here for a period of time, David and Emily bid farewell to their current colleagues, saying they were going to investigate elsewhere. Colleagues were not surprised or suspicious at this time because when David and Emily first arrived, they said that they had just come here from the age of dinosaurs hundreds of millions of years ago.

No one among their colleagues believed it, saying that it was even more bizarre than the myths. So, David and Emily took out the little dinosaur they brought with them from the dinosaur age hundreds of millions of years ago and showed it to everyone.

Colleagues were stunned. From then on, David and Emily were regarded as divine people, who were able to perform any miracle. Colleagues were reluctant to part with David and Emily, and hoped that they would have the opportunity to come back again in the future.

Chapter 2

THE INSECT WORLD

avid and Emily had experienced the first-hand environment at the age of dinosaurs. At that time, no human beings walked the Earth—it was truly a *"world without man."* But that was hundreds of millions of years ago. Today, "no man's world" not only refers to those planets that are still not suitable for human survival, but also refers to some planets where humans may survive, but no humans have yet appeared.

David and Emily used the Divine Watch to search for such planets in the Silver Way Galaxy, Universe B. They had found an unmanned planet. They named it Inset Star. There were actually no larger animals on this planet. There were only a few mice, small snakes, and small birds like sparrows there. This might be related to the ecological environment here. However, there were a lot of insects living on this planet. There are over one million species of insects on Earth. According to David's rough estimate, there were no less than one million species of insects on this planet. David discovered that there were many species of insects here that were not found on Earth.

The world of insects looked graceful and peaceful superficially.

In the summer days, it was warm and the land was full of vitality.

All kinds of insects made different calls. Cicadas on marks high trees made high-pitched sounds of "chi-le, chi-le." The grasshoppers on the ground made a sound like playing a pipa, and the crickets made a fricative sound like a harmonica.

Several kinds of insects emitted different tones, which were like harmonious music in an accompaniment harmony.

The melodious songs of the insects deeply touched the hearts of David and Emily.

David usually liked crickets, grasshoppers, locusts, dragonflies, and so on. Emily loved butterflies, bees, cicadas, moths, and more. She had also raised silkworms, finding them to be charming creatures—

though, mistakenly, she considered them mollusks.

David and Emily had some excess energy at this time. They wanted to lower their figures, to go deep into the insect world, to experience and investigate everything there carefully.

Using the Divine Watch and a Magic Spell, they shrank to the size of beetles and plunged into the vast sea of insects—tiny enough to go unnoticed—allowing them to conduct deeper observations and research. In the past, they shrunk to the size of dogs and cats at most. At this time, the two of them were like two crickets and were not noticeable in the animal world. They seemed to have turned into insects and blended themselves into the insect world.

In the eyes of David and Emily, the movements, postures, even expressions, and voices of each insect were immediately visible and vividly remembered. They could have a panoramic view of the interactions and even fights and killings between insects.

In this way, David and Emily came into close contact with all kinds of different insects, including beetles molluscs, flying insects, mud worms, and so on.

Insects are also full of competition. Not only among heterogeneous species, but even among the same kind they are not giving in to each other.

There were also *vicious* insects—centipedes, scorpions, venomous bees, cockroaches, mosquitoes, and flies—akin to the outlaws of the human world. Actually, they were insects with powerful weapons that were both defensive and offensive.

David and Emily each held a stick as a defensive weapon. First of all, they were faced with repeated attacks of mosquitoes and flies. The sizes of mosquitoes and flies were comparable to the reduced smaller bodies of David and Emily. To deal with the mosquitoes and flies that seemed huge at this time, they had to use great strength, just like driving away wolves that pounced on them. These hateful mosquitoes and flies made a deliberate buzzing sound, like bombers descending from the sky. They came back again and again, which was annoying. For safety, David and Emily took refuge in a secluded spot on higher ground, surrounded by green leaves on three sides—a place easy to defend and difficult to attack. They were here to observe everything around them and pay close attention to insects on the ground.

Here, they witnessed a wonderful duel between several crickets nearby. David immediately recognized a high-rate kind of cricket with a dark brown body that was flexible and vigorous, with a pair of crystal-clear and shiny wings on its back. His eyes were sparkling bright, and his limbs were tall and strong.

Several crickets took turns to fight the veteran. Emily called the veteran the conqueror, alluding to a brave warrior in ancient China. The contestants in this competition abided by the rules of the game. Each player took turns to fight against the overlord. The overlord had conquered all his opponents and won many battles, winning finally the dominance of the group arena. Of course, the duel was very fierce and tragic. Many players were injured in the battle. It was just that the other players were defeated one by one in the battle. The overlord won a great victory in the end. He fell down due to overexcitement and a serious leg injury. He struggled to get up from the ground, only to find that his right leg had been bitten off by the opponent's crickets during the fight.

At this moment, several ants hurriedly came forward, lifted him up, and put him on their shoulders. They transported the overlord to the ant nest and he became a delicious meal for the ant colony. In the eyes of David and Emily, the overlord was a tragic hero among crickets.

David and Emily saw a mother sparrow fly to the ground and dig a few times in the soil with her claws, then she pulled a small earthworm with her beak, pulled it out completely, and put it aside temporarily. She went on pulling out another one. After the bird had collected enough, she picked them up with her beak and flew back to her nest. There were a few baby birds in the nest chirping, waiting to be fed. Not only earthworms, but some soft-bodied wriggling worms were also delicacies for birds to feed their young.

In fact, grasshoppers, cicadas, and other insects were delicious, too, and they were all delicacies of some animals.

Once, David and Emily saw several dragonflies perched on the ground. The dragonflies here were roughly similar to those on Earth. However, they were larger and more colorful. The dragonfly's eyes were bulging like beads. It had three single eyes and two compound eyes, and each compound eye was composed of more than 28,000 small eyes. With such a staggering number of eyes, dragonflies naturally have the best eyesight of all.

One of the key reasons behind the dragonfly's exceptional flying skills is its remarkable eyesight. Its compound eyes provide nearly 360-degree vision, allowing it to see in all directions—front, back, above, and below—without needing to turn its head.

The head of the dragonfly is very large, the body is very slender, and there are four light and transparent wings growing on the back. Generally speaking, the dragonfly with its nice body shape can be called a model among insects.

David and Emily were amazed by the superb design of the dragonfly's beautiful and delicate body, the all-around eyes, and dexterous wings. They admired and worshiped the Almighty God.

David and Emily each mounted the back of a dragonfly, eager to soar through the air on these delicate, living aircraft. The two dragonflies flew up and circled in the air. The flight of a dragonfly was not as smooth and monotonous as that of an airplane but rather turned around from time to time and interspersed randomly in the air, up, down, left, and right. The flying speed of a dragonfly was ten meters per second, and its wings vibrated up to thirty or fifty times per second. David and Emily didn't feel dizzy in the dexterous plane of the dragonfly. They felt great.

When dragonflies flew over the water, they gently tapped their lower bodies on the surface in a motion known as *"water dipping."* In reality, this was their way of laying eggs into the water. Baby dragonflies grow in water. After molting, they left the water.

David and Emily rode separately on two dragonflies. At first, they could still see each other. Later, the dragonflies they were riding on flew in different directions, and each went on its own way. The two of them were a bit anxious. David wanted to search for Emily's whereabouts on the Divine Watch. He accidentally let go and fell off the back of the dragonfly. He fell into the water. David's Divine Watch was not lost because he usually hung it around his neck with a chain. Fortunately, David was a good swimmer. He swam to the shore, rested for a while, then looked around on the Divine Watch, and finally found Emily's location at this time.

The dragonfly Emily was riding on came to a tree branch on the shore. She stepped down from the dragonfly, looking for the lost David. Emily had no idea where David was at this moment. She shouted loudly, "David! David! Where are you?" She called several times but there was no answer. Later, she brainstormed and recited the Magic Spell. In a moment, the two unexpectedly walked together. They knew that their Divine Watch and Magic Spell helped them to reunite.

David and Emily had some berries to eat before going to explore elsewhere.

They strolled through the insect world with their tiny, beetle-like figures.

They once saw many white mollusks eating leaves in some bushes. Emily recognized these mollusks as silkworms on Earth.

Emily: Come on, David. There are silkworms here, how beautiful!

David: Yes. They are bigger than silkworms on Earth.

Emily: Yes. Let's call them Inset silkworms.

They grow on the planet of Inset.

David: I know you once raised silkworms. Emily: Yes. That's why I really like silkworms.

Look at them eating mulberry leaves. They keep eating, eating hard, day and night.

David: Why? Can't they rest and play for a while?

Emily: They are in a hurry to grow faster, become adults, and then spin silk to make cocoons.

David: And then what?

Emily: They turn into silkworm pupae in their own cocoons.

David: What happens after that?

Emily: The silkworm pupa turns into a moth. The silkworm moth bites through its cocoon and walks out of it.

David: And then what?

Emily: Then the male and female moths mate and the females lay seeds. Silkworm seeds are like grains of millet.

David: In a few days, the silkworm seeds will hatch into young silkworms, like little worms.

Emily: That's right. These little silkworms are starting to eat mulberry leaves again, starting a new generation of life.

David: Wow! This is so interesting. From small silkworms to large ones, to silkworm pupae, to silkworm moths and cubs. Each generation repeats itself like this, endlessly.

Emily: This is biology, the reproduction of biology.

In fact, all living things are like that.

David: All living things eat, grow, and reproduce.

Emily: But humans have more pursuits.

David: That's the biggest difference between humans and other organisms.

David and Emily drank some water in the stream, then they came to the front of a honeycomb.

Emily: I'm also very much interested in bees. Honey bees are a social group, they live a gregarious life. They collect pollen together, brew and store honey together, and pass the flowerless period together.

David: Bees only eat pollen and they have to store enough honey for the winter when there are no flowers. Bees give us a sense of diligence because they must seize the flowering season.

Emily: I admire the hard work of the bees.

David: But more importantly, bees have a very close relationship with human life. Most of the crops and fruit trees planted by humans rely on bees to pollinate them to reproduce. There is a prediction in the world: if bees disappear from the earth, human beings can only survive for four years. Some scientists are concerned that, at the current rate of bee disappearance, around 40,000 plant species in nature will struggle with reproduction, potentially facing extinction. This, in turn, could lead to widespread food shortages for humanity.

Emily: Wow! It turns out that bees are friends and benefactors of human beings.

David and Emily had not only seen the above interesting things in the insect world, but also focused on the activities of ants.

Ants have three distinct body parts: the head, thorax, and abdomen. The front of the head houses a pair of compound eyes and a pair of antennae. Movement is powered by three pairs of legs attached to the thorax.

Ants build nests in the soil, with strong limbs and agile walking. They rely on their strong physique and group strength to defeat some insects that are countless times larger than them. Some sick or injured large insects, such as crickets and locusts, often become the captives or trophies of ants. They are carried back to the ant nest by several ants, dedicated to the ant queen, or used as food reserves.

Ants have a long lifespan. Worker ants and ant queens can live up to ten years.

Ants are a typical social group. Each group is organized in an orderly manner.

Individuals of the same species can cooperate with each other to take care of the larvae. There is a clear division of labor. There can be at least two overlapping generations in the ant colony, and the younger generation can take care of the older generation for a period of time. Ants are considered the most hardworking and disciplined creatures on Earth, as well as the most intelligent insects. They are probably the same on Inset Star.

In ecosystems, the relationship between ants and aphids fluctuates between symbiosis, reciprocity, and development. When aphids and ants have a symbiotic relationship, both ants and aphids can benefit from this relationship.

Emily suggested they search for the interactions between ants and aphids. They combed through various plants, and after much searching, they finally discovered the scene they had been hoping for.

They saw ants running up and down busily along the stem of the plant. On the leaves, they saw some ants as well as some aphids. The ants touched the aphids occasionally and got the stuff they needed, just like the people who got milk from the cows.

Emily: No one would have imagined that ants would raise cows and milk like humans. This is true, but ants raise aphids and squeeze honeydew from them.

David: Aphids rely on plant sap for survival. They use the "needle tube" on their mouths to pierce the outer skin of plants, suck up plant juice, digest it, and then secrete a shiny viscous substance called "honeydew".

Emily: Look, what are they doing?

David: Oh, I see. The ants are milking the aphids. The ants are using their antennae to *massage* the abdomen of the aphids, stimulating them to expel honey.

Emily: This honeydew contains a lot of sugar and serves as an energy source for ants and other aphid predators.

David: The ants feed on the honeydew, and in return, they protect the aphids from predators. Aphids rely on ants for protection, and ants rely on aphids for sustenance.

Emily: Therefore, a mutually adaptive symbiotic relationship.

The group sociality of ants and the symbiotic relationship between ants and aphids made David and Emily ponder and be fascinated. This is undoubtedly the exquisite design and arrangement of Heaven. Animals are not just harmonious or hostile, and the relationship between groups and symbiosis is close to that between humans.

However, ants also have their natural enemies.

There is an anteater that eats ants.

Its mouth is tube-shaped, and its tongue is retractable and mucus-rich, suitable for licking small insects. It feeds on ants. When the anteater comes, the ants will suffer huge losses. Why God created this natural enemy for ants is a difficult question to answer. That day, David and Emily watched a fierce ant war on an open field. This was a life-and-death struggle between two ant colonies for the ownership of a nesting site. Both warring parties mobilized thousands of large forces. The soldiers fought desperately, biting the enemy's thin neck with their teeth, like steel pliers, and beheading the enemy's heads. Sometimes three or four ants bit together, and their courage to kill the enemy and the spirit to face death calmly were no less than human warriors.

The stumped limbs and arms of the slain enemy, and the countless bitten heads of ants scattered on the ground of the battlefield, like a bunch of black rice spread on the ground. Beautiful flowers, butterflies, and bees nestled within them have long been symbols of grace, often evoking a poetic and artistic imagery in the minds of people.

Once, while Emily was indulging in admiring a large flower with beauty and fragrance, several bees who came to collect honey also fell there. Emily felt very happy, with the surroundings aroused her romantic feelings. At this moment she was on par with the bee in proportion to her figure. She approached a honey bee and touched it. Unexpectedly, the bee raised her butt and stung Emily on the facc. Emily felt a sharp pain, screamed, and fell to the ground. At this time, David was watching some butterflies in the distance and ran quickly to Emily when he saw the event. He tripped over the gravel in a hurry and fell down. He was seriously injured and lying on the ground without getting up for a while.

A group of ants who were looking for food swarmed up, without any explanation, picked up David and Emily, and quickly transported them to their nest. David and Emily cried out as they struggled. At this time, their own destinies were controlled by these small insects. It was absurd to think about it, but they could only blame themselves. If they hadn't shrunk their bodies and joined the insect group, how could they have found themselves in this dire situation?

After their figures were reduced, David had already set the index of restoring their original figure on the Divine Watch. They could easily get away and return to their original heights just by reciting the Magic Spell by Emily in an emergency. David called out to Emily, "Emily, hurry up, cast the Spell!" Emily then read the Magic Spell. David and Emily immediately returned to their original figures. They brushed away a few small ants attached to their bodies with the palms of their hands.

In retrospect, it was a dangerous event. They were almost dragged into the ant nest and became a feast for the ants.

David and Emily had once deeply admired the bravery, tenacity, collectivism, and self-sacrificing spirit of ants. However, they themselves were ambushed by ants and almost lost their lives in the ant nest. Can it be said that this is the injustice or evil of ants? It seems that human standards of right

and wrong, good and evil, cannot be applied
to animals.

Chapter 3

THE JUNGLE WORLD

avid and Emily searched on the Divine Watch and found an uninhabited planet with all kinds of creatures. They called it Janger. But that was on the time coordinate of 10 million years ago.

The climate there was mild, and most of the land was covered by virgin tropical forests. David and Emily thought it was a fascinating place. They decided to go to this *no man's world* to experience it by themselves.

David determined the position of Janger on the Divine Watch, and Emily gave a signal with a Magic Spell. In an instant, the two arrived at Janger.

David and Emily found themselves in a brand-new environment. This was a primitive ecology somewhat similar to the dinosaur era. Due to the mild climate and abundant water, the plants here grew exceptionally lush, and there was also a wide variety of animals, lively and energetic. In this *no man's world*, flowers were blooming and birds were singing everywhere. Springs, rivers, and lakes were all over the land. The land was covered by green grasses and beautiful wildflowers dotted among them. Hares, goats, and deer of different breeds ran happily on the grassland, stopping to graze from time to time. Swarms of sparrows and swallows flew low. The air was clean, and the wildland emitted the intoxicating fragrance of flowers and plants.

In the clear river, one could see swimming fish, as well as groups of tadpoles and green frogs. *How elegant and poetic it all looked*! David and Emily strolled on this charming and beautiful prairie, and it seemed that some beautiful music sounded in their ears, making them relaxed and happy.

Various trees, shrubs, and climbing plants grew in the primeval forest. There were many kinds of towering trees. When one looked up, one could hardly see the top of the trees. There were many kinds of broad-leaved and coniferous trees as well as various kinds of mushroom, agaric, and other fungus plants on the ground and tree trunks. All the plants here were competing for sunlight, water, and nutrition for their own growth. Individual plants did not give in to each other. David and Emily witnessed the survival competition of plants. That was quite fierce.

What was the situation between animals?

There is a Chinese idiom, *"When a mantis catches a cicada, a yellow finch is behind"*. It is said that a mantis trying to kill a cicada while an oriole is behind its back. The praying mantis fails to catch the cicada, but is caught by the oriole. This is mainly a comparison of strengths. The mantis cannot catch the cicada, but it can only be caught by the yellow finch. The yellow finch may be killed by a poisonous snake one day. And that poisonous snake may be swallowed by a crocodile.

The law of bullying is the "jungle law".

It is not uncommon for lions, tigers, and leopards to chase deer and antelope, and to attack wild beasts and bisons, killing and sharing their meat and offal.

David and Emily saw two small antelopes hiding in the bushes when they walked in the wilderness. It seemed that they had just been born and were still waiting for their mother to nurse them. Emily picked up a small antelope, which bleated and was very cute. David found some tender leaves to feed them, and they actually started chewing. Every day thereafter, David and Emily came to visit them. These two antelopes grew very fast and began to search for edible grass around themselves. However, their mother, an adult antelope, still came home every day to feed their children. This kind of maternal love deeply touched the hearts of David and Emily.

Later, the mother antelope never came back. She had tried to graze as much as possible on the grassland, hoping to produce more milk for her growing children. But the mother antelope was attacked by a powerful cheetah, killed, and dragged back to its den.

The cheetah family shared all of the meat and internal organs of the antelope. All that remained was but a pile of bones and fur.

A couple of days later when David and Emily passed by the antelope's home in the bushes again, the two little antelopes were missing. They saw some blood stains on the nearby grass, and it was estimated that one or both of the antelopes had also been killed. The tragedy on the grassland left David and Emily speechless. They stood at the scene of the tragedy with heavy hearts, unable to leave for a long time.

On another occasion, David and Emily saw a cow and her three calves besieged by a pack of hyenas who, relying on their large number, attempted to capture the calves, kill them, and share the beef. The cow fought hard and arched from left to right, never allowing the calves to be harmed. But the hyenas stalked and fought fiercely, leaving the cattle struggling to cope. Hyenas are a type of beast with repulsive appearance and habits. David and Emily deeply sympathized with the difficult situation of the cow and her calves. But they were unable to reach out and rescue the trapped bison. Later, the cow appeared exhausted from the frantic fight with the hyenas, and she was panting heavily. When a calf was knocked down by several hyenas, the cow went all out to rescue the calf. She was injured in many places and still did not give up.

At that moment, four bisons charged in to their rescue. Together, they scattered the hyenas and stabbed one particularly daring hyena with their horns. In this way, the cow and her three calves were saved, escorted back to the herd by the river. David and Emily cheered for the escape of the trapped cow and three calves.

The cow, who was wounded in many places in saving the calves, suffered from wound ulcers and exhaustion, died in a fight with the lions.

She was bitten on the neck and thrown to the ground, and several lions tore her flesh and internal organs. The cow became the underdog and the prey of the strong.

However, in the competitive arena of the jungle, even the king of beasts such as lions, tigers, and leopards cannot always maintain their dominant position. They are attacked by different species in groups, such as hounds, or suffer losses in the same kind. When the animal king is old, he will be driven out of the herd by the younger and more promising new animal king, and it is often tragic to find a lonely place to die.

David and Emily saw the living conditions of living things in this primitive ecological environment. Behind the beautiful natural scenery, there was fierce competition for survival.

In close observation, the reproduction of organisms was full of fierce games, life-and-death struggles, and ferocious murderous intentions against competitors.

The survival of the biological world depends on *strength* and *force*. The competition was brutal and merciless. The so-called "scent of flowers and singing of birds" and "warblers sing and swallows dance" actually only exist in some people's beautiful dreams. In nature, there is only ruthlessness under the cover of gentle appearance.

David and Emily wanted to leave the era of no-man's world.

They were curious and wanted to see what this beautiful place would look like in the future. It was just like the last time when they watched the change of the same place over hundreds of millions of years from the age of dinosaurs.

David identified in the Divine Watch a "human world" thousands of years later. Emily gave the order with a Spell. The two of them stayed in the original place, and the place became completely different in an instant.

The most important thing was that an unmanned world had become a human society. Human beings as higher-developed animals became the natural masters of the biological world. Human beings dominated all living creatures on Earth, even the once-ferocious beasts like lions and tigers, because they possessed weapons and wisdom far surpassing the brute force and sharp claws of these animals.

All animals, including those crawling on the ground, those flying in the sky, and those swimming in the water, obediently submit to the lewdness of human beings. Humans could consume them and enslave them according to their own needs and will.

The wild horses became war horses or chariot horses, and the soldiers galloped across the battlefield on horseback, fighting hard. *How many war horses died on the battlefield!* Wild boars became domestic pigs, the main source of meat for human food. The pheasant became a domestic chicken.

The rooster crowed in the morning, and the hen laid eggs. Eggs became an important food for people.

At this time, Janger Star had changed from a world with a beautiful natural environment, full of competing creatures to a place where humans enslaved other animals, and the law of the jungle was implemented more terribly than in the uninhabited world. In fact, the emergence of human beings has brought disasters and endless suffering to other types of organisms.

The meat food of Humans was mainly beef, pork, chicken, and fish. This reminded David and Emily of the ant's natural enemy, the anteater. Anteaters feed on ants. Humans eat beef, pork, chicken, and fish in large quantities. So, humans are actually bull-eaters, pig-eaters, chicken-eaters, and fish-eaters. Moreover, humans also breed cattle, pigs, chickens, and in captivity, producing a large amount of animal meat.

The cruelty of human beings towards other animals is appalling.

Humans raise some cattle, only to eat their meat. The capitalists crowd many cattle in the breeding pen in cattle farms, in order to promote the growth of cattle as fast as possible and gain higher profits. Each cow is confined to a narrow space, with nowhere to lie down except for standing and eating feed. The meat ducks are forced to eat or even stuffed artificially, in order to promote their fast growth and eat their meat as soon as possible.

Such growth-promoting methods lower the quality of animal meat. As a result, edible meat and meat products lose value in the market, sometimes even falling below the price of vegetables. This, in turn, creates a vicious cycle—leading to even more breeding and mass slaughter of livestock.

People eat almost all kinds of animals on land, sea, and air, and various delicacies, all based on meat.

Many people enjoy hunting wild animals as a hobby, not necessarily to eat the meat of their prey.

All animals are subject to and driven by people. Humans can capture and hunt them in the wild fields at any time. Even lions, tigers, monkeys, crocodiles, and hippopotamuses, the kings of beasts, are forced to stay in zoo cages for people to watch.

The meat of various animals is always indispensable on the human table. Animals are slaughtered and their meat is processed into various meat foods. Today's human beings have fully adapted to the habit of using animal meat as food. The meat processing industry and the fast-food industry based on beef, pork, and chicken are enduring.

People have long been accustomed to such cruelties and are indifferent. Even benevolent and kind old people, gentle women, and innocent children are no exception. When people eat delicious animal meat, few of them will think that they are actually like ferocious beasts chewing the meat of other poor hunted animals, dripping with blood and steaming, and emitting a smell or odor of blood and flesh.

What a ruthless jungle law, what a hypocritical humanitarian spirit!

In order to obtain precious ivory as a material for making luxurious decorations, people do not hesitate to hunt and kill elephants living well on the grassland in large numbers. The mighty elephant loses its precious life simply because its tusks are deemed valuable by some. Its massive body lies lifeless on the open grassland, a haunting and desolate sight. In this, the arrogance, cruelty, and ruthless exploitation of humanity are laid bare.

Compared with the uninhabited world in the prehistoric era of Janger, how different is the human world today? David and Emily have witnessed the law of the jungle including the insect world on the Inset Star. David and Emily discovered to their disappointment that human beings had not only followed the law of the jungle in the uninhabited world, but also carried it forward, and their cruelty to other animals far exceeded the law of the jungle rules among other animals.

One night, David and Emily had a dream at the same time. Their dreams were roughly the same. That was, they fell into the hands of animals enslaved by humans and were brought to justice by the animals.

David and Emily were put in jail. The prison conditions were extremely poor, like a water cell. It seemed that this was also a punishment for human crimes. They were submerged in a pool of stinky water, which was full of maggots crawling up and down, and the stench was overwhelming. There were also numerous green-headed flies flying to harass and continue to lay eggs in the smelly water.

Some big and fat maggots crawled on them. It made them feel sick and nauseating. This might be the punishment that evil human beings deserve.

David: We were accidentally taken into prisons. Prisoners shouldn't be abused, they should at least have some humanity, right?

Emily: David, don't forget where we are now. People talk about humanity and the like. Have people talk to animals about that?

David: Exactly. People are too hypocritical.

Emily: We deserve what we are treated today.

On the day when David and Emily were interrogated, they were surrounded by a large number of animals, and they were regarded as representatives of human beings for the persecution of animals, to be denounced and accused.

A cow came forward, full of snot and tears, accusing human beings of the cruel persecution of his relatives for dozens of generations. Each generation of cows was forced to work hard until they grew old, often sweating profusely, and were whipped and beaten severely. When they were old and weak, they were slaughtered and eaten, added directly to dishes, or processed into various beef products. The cowhide was peeled off and processed into leather products. Not even the horns and bones were spared. Which cow did not have a bitter tear in her heart, blood on her body, and hatred in her heart? Before the emergence of human beings, the lives of cattle had been much better. At most, a few were eaten by lions and tigers. Most of the bison lived in style, eating grass in the wild, and could rest at any time.

A lot of pigs, chickens, as well as fish in the water, also competed to speak and complain. Due to time constraints, the complaints had to come to an end temporarily.

Humans were outraged in the animal kingdom. David and Emily, as representatives of human beings, were pushed to the forefront. The Animal Kingdom formed a makeshift judicial committee, appointing a horse, a rhino, and an ostrich to pass judgment on David and Emily for their crimes. It showed that consciously or unconsciously, David and Emily participated in human persecution of animals, eating animal meat and using animal leather products, countless murders were involved. They were sentenced to serious crimes. Combined punishment for several crimes, both were sentenced to death. Defense attorneys, an owl, and a giraffe disputed the ruling. They pointed out that carnivorous animals in the animal kingdom such as tigers, lions, and leopards committed life-long crimes and involved a large number of murders, so how to deal with them?

The owl said that the rules of life in the animal world were not made by the animals themselves. From their birth, the world had been like this.

So, it was unfair to punish only human beings who bullied animals. All living beings should be equal before the law. The horse who was the Chief Justice said that there was nothing we could do about the relationship between animals. We had to wait for the future. Maybe God would have a brilliant strategy to handle it in the future.

In this way, David and Emily were released on bail pending trial. They bore a shameful charge for mankind, inevitably feeling guilty. It was a complete hypocrite to think that although human beings claimed to be civilized, they did all kinds of evil to animals. In addition to the enslavement and killing of other animals by humans, wasn't it the case among human beings?

The wars of humankind are battles of brute force, where the strong prevail through ruthlessness. In the end, the victor becomes the prince, while the defeated is condemned as the bandit. Large-scale wars kill and injure millions and tens of millions of young soldiers. Using lethal weapons, the battlefield is far more tragic than the battle between ant colonies. Even in peacetime, dictators' perverse and reckless actions will cause a large number of civilian casualties.

In human society, we progress toward civilization by upholding the rule of law, fostering transparent governance, and embracing the values of equality, friendship, morality, and humanism. This will help mankind get rid of the competition law of bullying.

After David and Emily woke up from the nightmare, they seemed to feel even clearer than before. They discussed the issue of the jungle law.

Emily: David, we are currently on the battlefield of biological competition.

Firstly, there were uninhabited primitive wilderness and jungles, followed by the world in which human beings participated. There is always the rule of the jungle in between, and in the world after the emergence of humanity, the situation of bullying seems to be intensifying.

David: Yes. The law of the jungle originated from the primitive biological world. Human beings are intelligent and advanced creatures and should have developed towards a higher civilized society, using more rational and fair principles to handle the relationships between humans and animals, and even trying to adjust the relationships between animals to achieve harmonious coexistence.

Emily: This is too idealistic. There are many things that are ordained by God. Human beings are helpless.

David: Why are there strong and weak animals? Lions, tigers, and leopards are always strong and aggressive. Deer, sheep, and rabbits are always the weak, usually the oppressed and the victimized.

Emily: This kind of strength and weakness is innate. It's not their fault.

David: Deer, sheep, and rabbits can only survive by their ability to escape. Those who run fast can survive. Those who run slowly are eliminated. In addition, deer, sheep, and rabbits have strong fertility, which is also a condition for the survival of vulnerable animals. This is the regulation of acquired and external factors, also known as *"external limitation"* in the law of *"creation by Heaven and Earth."*

Emily: There is another saying called *'maintaining ecological balance'*. This is to use dominant animals to suppress the excessive reproduction of weaker animals. Just like the reintroduction of wolves in Yellowstone Park in the United States to control the overpopulation of deer.

David: So, God created powerful animals such as lions, tigers, and leopards based on this consideration. Yeah?

Emily: If this principle were introduced into human society, it would not be so reasonable. Can the presence of strong groups suppress the over-expansion of vulnerable groups?

David: The matter is far from so simple.

Emily: Right. However, I still don't quite understand why God creates the strong and the weak in the first place? This isn't fair, right?

David: What you mean by 'fairness' is probably just our human philosophy. We cannot understand and demand that God obey humanity.

Emily: Yes. God's actions are mysterious and unpredictable. Human beings will never reach it.

Chapter 4

THE WATER WORLD

David and Emily traveled to Orson, a planet mostly covered with water.

The two settled down on the only piece of land here. This land was like an isolated island surrounded by a vast ocean. Due to the mild climate, there were lush plants and countless kinds of animals growing on this land. Most of the animals and plants that existed on the Earth were found here. There were all kinds of terrestrial animals on the land, and countless colorful aquatic animals and plants in the water. Among them were some unknown and strange plants and animals that had never been seen on Earth.

When they first came to the continent of Orson, David and Emily got acquainted with several animals, one of them was a tiger here. They had intersected with dinosaurs that were bigger than tigers, so they were not afraid of tigers. They called this tiger "Victor". Victor usually liked to snuggle on David and Emily and made purring sounds like a cat to express his comfort when he was happy, he would lick the hands and faces of

David and Emily with his tongue. David and Emily stroke his fur. The earthy yellow fur had regular dark patterns and glittered in the sunlight. In the eyes of David and Emily, wasn't this a big cat?

David and Emily especially liked the water here. Whether it was the fresh water in the lake or the seawater in the sea, it was so clear. At times, the two would gaze at the underwater scene for long moments, mesmerized by the shifting colors and fluid movements. Beautiful fish glided gracefully through the waters, transforming it into a shimmering crystal palace—enchanting and utterly captivating.

How David and Emily hoped to swim underwater and appreciate the charm of the "crystal palace"! David switched and tested different parameters on his Divine Watch, and finally found a function that allowed him and Emily to change themselves and adapt to the underwater environment. This function modified the physical conditions of David and Emily so that they could stay and survive underwater for a long time without causing discomfort. Their vital capacity had been increased and their body shape had become close to streamlined. Their respiratory organs became able to temporarily stop breathing without suffocation, not breathing through nostrils for a long time, and could resist the pressure of water in the depth of water.

David looked at the changed Emily, a bit like a mermaid in a fairy tale.

David: Emily, you look so beautiful!

Emily: Oh, I'm almost forty years old.

David: Now you look like you're in your twenties.

Emily: David, you don't know how interesting you look now. Like a male mermaid. A fish has the head of a Greek god. The two laughed.

After the launch was ready, David made adjustments and confirmations on the Divine Watch. David and Emily took off their coats, each wearing only a pair of shorts. Then Emily issued the order with the

Magic Spell, and the two of them dived into the water together.

David and Emily felt as if they had stepped into an entirely new world. The vibrant, dazzling beauty of the underwater realm made their journey feel truly worthwhile.

The aquatic plants of various colors and shapes under the water were gently rippling with the water waves. Different species of fish swam back and forth in the clear water, interspersed among the aquatic plants, as if playing a game of hide-and-seek. David and Emily swam freely underwater like fish. Besides the fish, they also saw jellyfish and squid. The jellyfish looked like umbrella covers, with hands and legs of uneven length growing out from under the umbrella covers. The jellyfish danced in the water, the scene was quite poetic.

David and Emily saw several kinds of shrimp in the water. They moved cunningly and changeably, sometimes paddling quickly, sometimes jumping and churning.

It had a completely different demeanor from fish. Crabs had a unique style. They always had their own hiding places at the bottom of the water, and they appeared and disappeared from time to time. When they acted, they tended to move to one side, so it was called "sidewise moving – riding roughshod", which was why people often said "rampage". As for turtles and tortoises, their movements were somewhat similar to those of crabs, they seldom showing up. Their gait was different from that of crabs, always walking slowly and looking around. When it saw something unusual, it immediately shrank its head, known as a "shrinking turtle".

David and Emily met some dolphins underwater. These dolphins swam freely in the water, turning up and down, left and right, and interspersed effortlessly. They were said to be highly intelligent. Two dolphins saw David and Emily and ran over to say hello to the newcomers. David and Emily ran their hands over them, and they rolled happily in the water. Although they could not exchange information with each other, there seemed to be a resonance, or telepathy, between humans and dolphins. Feelings could be exchanged between them. David and Emily made friends with the two dolphins underwater. They named the two friends "Yilan" and "Yida" respectively.

David and Emily often met with Yilan and Yida in the water. They let David and Emily ride on their backs. It was like riding horses, galloping in the water. The two dolphins sometimes submerged and sometimes surfaced. David and Emily felt more dashing than riding a horse on land. Horses usually only ran on flat ground, while dolphins could roll up and down, left and right.

Once, while taking an underwater walk, David and Emily came across a crocodile with a big crab in his mouth. The crab was about to become the crocodile's lunch. He was desperately trying to break free from the crocodile's mouth, but it was difficult to succeed.

David and Emily pulled the crab out of the crocodile's mouth. Although the crab lost a leg, he survived.

David and Emily called it Crab Klapp.

David and Emily often watched underwater crocodiles, which were amphibious animals, often diving into the water. It had a layer of hard skin all over its body, with rough bumps on it, like armor for self-defense. Its long mouth was full of sharp teeth.

It had a strong bite. It took David and Emily a lot of effort to rescue the crab from the mouth of a crocodile. It was David who was quick-witted and kicked the crocodile's mouth to save the crab.

Seeing the image and every movement of the crocodile, David and Emily naturally recalled the dinosaurs on Dasor Star hundreds of millions of years ago. It was said that crocodiles evolved from swimming dinosaurs. They saw that the shape and action of crocodiles were quite similar to those of swimming dinosaurs back then. They were more convinced that some of the swimming dinosaurs were later influenced by different environments and evolved into crocodiles.

Of course, crocodiles were by no means nice guys in the animal world. They preyed on smaller, weaker animals, using their amphibious abilities to launch stealthy attacks on those drinking at the water's edge. Their swift, calculated movements made them highly effective predators—striking successfully nine times out of ten.

The crocodile here didn't hurt David and Emily. David and Emily didn't seem to care too much about the danger of crocodiles. They regarded crocodiles as the descendants of dinosaurs. When dinosaurs were alive, they made friends with them. David and Emily never forget the old relationship of crocodile ancestors. The underwater world was not always quiet and all animals got along well. If one watched carefully enough, one might notice that it was not peaceful there.

If the small fish was not careful enough, it would be swallowed by the sudden attack of the big fish. People often said, "Big fish eat small fish, and small fish eat shrimps," a truth that reflects the harsh "jungle law" of the underwater world. This law led to brutal massacres and the cruel loss of lives among the aquatic creatures. Some fierce fish, such as sharks, even eat other fish for a living, just like large carnivores on land. If it did not do this, it would starve itself to death. In this regard, on the land and underwater were basically the same.

Once, David and Emily, guests from land to underwater tourism, witnessed a terrifying scene.

David and Emily were walking underwater, and while they were talking, they suddenly heard a terrifying cry from some nearby fish.

It was here to warn the fish to be careful, a shark was coming. They saw all kinds of fish and shrimp in a panic, fleeing and seeking refuge. David and Emily also wanted to hide, but found nowhere to hide. They were quick-witted and acted in a hurry. David enlarged their figures by adjusting on the Divine Watch. Emily quickly gave an order. The two of them suddenly became giants, with their upper bodies protruding from the water. When the shark approached and saw the two large creatures, it quickly realized it couldn't take them on. With a swift turn, it veered away, searching for easier prey.

Another time, David and Emily were watching a beautiful aquatic plant underwater. The aquatic plant seemed to stretch out some beautiful arms to the viewers. The clusters of arms were soft and delicate, swaying with the water waves, as if calling people to go into its gentle and friendly embrace.

David and Emily approached these arms and watched them carefully. These arms immediately embraced them warmly. When David and Emily wanted to end the hug and go elsewhere, they found that they were tightly entangled by those arms, making them unable to extricate themselves.

It turned out that these seemingly harmless aquatic plants were actually underwater creatures, camouflaged to lure in unsuspecting visitors. Once close enough, they would capture their prey and swallow them whole. David and Emily realized that they had been cheated. Their bodies were getting more and more tightly bound, and they had become something in another one's pocket, a meal in its mouth.

Emily: David! Divine Watch, Divine Watch!

David: Oops, my arm is entangled and I can't adjust the watch.

At another moment, David and Emily were relieved. The dreadful arms that had wrapped them loosened. They saw that a big crab saved them. The crab used his powerful knife-shaped grippers to cut off the horrible arms that wrapped around them one by one, restoring their freedom.

David and Emily found that it was their friend Klapp who rescued them.

David and Emily thanked their savior, crab Klapp.

The crab said, "You are welcome. You are my benefactors." Then he left.

Sometime later, when David and Emily met crab Klapp again at the bottom of the sea, Klapp warmly invited them to visit his house. David and Emily felt that the hospitality was hard to decline, but they were also a little embarrassed. Klapp's house was under some large stones, The space was narrow, how could they get in?

David and Emily had a conversation underwater with gestures and expressions.

Emily: Well, David. Couldn't we solve this problem if we lowered our stature with the Divine Watch?

David: That's right. Let me tune up our watch. Okay. Please give an order, Emily.

As soon as Emily gave the order, the two became smaller together. It ended up being about the size of crab Klapp.

David and Emily followed crab Klapp to the rocks at the bottom of the sea. Those stones looked like some huge stone pillars. Emily called them Greek temples.

David and Emily seemed to come to an underwater world. They saw a dazzling array of things here. There were all kinds of mussels and mollusks. Among them, David recognized the invaluable pearl mussels containing precious pearls and the high-end food sea cucumbers. There were endless pearl mussels here. David and Emily felt like they had found a diamond mine with rich reserves. If these treasures were collected in large quantities, they would bring huge wealth with them, and David and Emily would become extremely rich. However, they did not value these things. They were definitely not going to explore the aliens for material interests. So, they felt like Alibaba, even less lucky than Alibaba with regard to wealth. They just came to the treasure house by chance and opened their eyes. They had no interest in taking wealth for themselves.

Moreover, even with the help of the Divine Watch, they couldn't transport wealth back to Earth. God didn't give any green light for them to make money.

When David talked about the precious pearl mussels and sea cucumbers, Emily thought it was too vulgar. Humans just knew to eat animals or to earn money with animals.

David agreed with Emily and felt that his words were inappropriate.

David and Emily followed Crab Klapp as they roamed the underwater palace. It was simply a luxurious palace. Underground was a beautiful and colorful carpet of soft seaweed. A wide variety of aquatic plants and animals were hung on the huge stone walls and pillars nearby. Some of them were glittering. In particular, the orange, green, and blue light luminous bodies were like crystal clear gemstones embedded in midair. Above, umbrella-shaped jellyfish were floating lightly, and some jellyfish could still emit light. The soft light was bright enough to illuminate this underwater palace.

The masters here were turtles and crabs. There were also beautiful tropical fish visiting and wandering in the clear water. The colors on those tropical fish were pleasing to the eye and soft, with stripes and color patches joining together to create a natural beauty, almost the work of a talented artist. Emily thought that this natural beauty should be designed from Heaven. It seemed that God had super high artistic talent.

They lingered a little in the treasure house. Finally, they thought of saying goodbye to Crab Klapp and walking out of the stone forest treasure house.

David and Emily had spent several days at the glamorous Crystal Palace.

One day, the bright sun shone into the sea. The scenery in the water was extremely beautiful.

Emily was unusually cheerful underwater. She closed her mouth and hummed a cheerful "Blue Danube Waltz" in her throat, involuntarily dancing her mermaid-like body. David, the male mermaid, danced to the same melody.

Several dolphins swimming nearby also moved up and down, singing along with their voices. Among them were their good friends Yilan and Yida. They spent a wonderful time dancing with their half-human, half-fish friends, David and Emily.

After this dance and music, it was followed by a more cheerful music "*Spring is Coming*" and a bolder Latin dance.

There was also more rapid and dynamic rhythmic jazz music and dance…

This joyful atmosphere infected a large number of residents in the water. More and more fish, shrimp, jellyfish, and squid were joining in, while Crab Klapp and several other crabs moved sideways in the water, with a unique style.

A group of happy turtles were swimming in the water.

Three crocodiles got excited and danced in the water with the steps of all the dancers, diving and surfacing.

The squids were taunting the crocodiles, deliberately releasing black ink in front of them to block their vision and disorient them.

Unexpectedly, at this time, a giant fish was passing by here. This giant fish was bigger than the largest whale in the big ocean on Earth. Seeing a large number of fish gathering, he thought it was a good opportunity for him to hunt. The giant fish was not polite, opened his mouth wide, and took most of the dancers into his belly. Some fanatical dancers continued to dance in the belly of the giant fish, and their passion was hard to dissipate.

David and Emily, who were also sucked into the belly of the fish, calmly realized their current situation. They had become prey in the belly of the giant fish, awaiting digestion and absorption, ultimately transforming into the flesh and blood of the predator—or, in time, into its waste.

The only way for David and Emily to get out of this dilemma was to resort to the Divine Watch and the Magic Spell. Because this artifact only exerted its magic power on its holders, it could do nothing for other dancers who were swallowed in the belly of the giant fish.

David and Emily had no choice but to say goodbye to them.

David set the destination on the Divine Watch, and in a hurry, he randomly selected a place on the land, and Emily issued a Magic Spell. The two disappeared from the belly of the fish.

When they arrived at the destination, they saw a wild mountain in front of them. The mermaid-like figures of David and Emily in the water disappeared automatically when they returned to the shore and returned to their original shapes. But because they took off their clothes before going into the water, they were still naked now.

They were already a little embarrassed to be naked. Looking around, they found that they were surrounded by a group of wolves that were approaching them step by step. Those bloodthirsty beasts were starving. How could they let go of the delicious meal in front of them? David and Emily thought that they had a feeling of "just coming out of the tiger's mouth and then going into the wolf's den". The eyes of those wolves flashed fierce light, showing bloodthirsty teeth and tongue. A wolf suddenly rushed up and bit David's arm. Emily was also attacked by several hungry wolves. She kept shouting, "Divine Watch, Divine Watch!" with his arm being seized by wolves, David could not use his Divine Watch to get out of trouble.

At this moment, a handsome tiger appeared in front of them, rushed to the wolf who was biting David, grabbed the wolf's neck with his big mouth, and then tossed it back and forth. Soon two of the wolves were out of breath. At this time, the other wolves gradually dispersed. The tiger abandoned the dying wolves and came to get close to David and Emily. It turned out that this was their good friend Victor.

David and Emily were deeply grateful for Victor's timely help and embraced the tiger tightly. In response, Victor gently licked them both with his large, warm tongue.

At this time, David and Emily realized that they were both naked because they took off their clothes and placed them on the shore before going into the water. Now they must return to the shore by the water and put on their clothes. They didn't know how far they had to go to get back to the original place near the water. David searched the map shown on the Divine Watch and finally found the place. However, the distance was too long to walk there. They had to reach this destination with the help of the Divine Watch.

So, they hugged the tiger Victor and bid farewell to him. David confirmed the location on the Divine Watch, Emily gave the Spell, and the two of them disappeared from the wilderness in an instant without a trace. Victor felt both baffled and a little lost.

In an instant, David and Emily came to the shore where they had launched into the water before and found their clothes. At this time, David and Emily realized that modern humans must wear clothes on land, which was very different from early humans.

David and Emily looked at the place where they danced with the aquatic animals in the water not long ago. They saw a lot of fish feces floating in the sea. There were also fish bones, fish scales, dolphin skins, and so on. So, this was the carnival group of fish that was eaten by the giant fish that day. They were dancers who danced with David and Emily. They were swallowed and digested by the giant fish and now turned into fish feces. David and Emily were both sad and guilty. These fish were inspired by David and Emily to dance together. These droppings of the large fish floating on the water became food for some small fish.

They competed to chase and devour these ready-made delicacies.

The big fish that devoured the dancers died suddenly due to overeating and indigestion and being attacked by another big fish. He had been stranded on the shore, his carcass washed up by the storm. His body was quickly scavenged by several packs of wild animals and vultures, leaving only scant remnants behind. Besides, the residue was also rotten, attracting many flies to chase the stink, and maggots crawling all over the ground. This is nature.

Chapter 5

THE BIRD WORLD

avid and Emily decided to explore a planet inhabited by a large number of birds called Berde. It was also an unmanned world before the emergence of human beings there.

The main inhabitants of the island were birds. David and Emily were the first humans to set foot on the island. They found all kinds of birds on the island. In addition to those species on Earth, there were many birds that they had never seen.

Here, they had seen pigeons, sparrows, crows, magpies, cuckoos, thrushes, etc., as well as chickens, ducks, geese, etc., but they were not poultry, but wild species.

There was a kind of small bird on this planet, similar to the sparrows on Earth. Because the small birds were light and mobile, their food and water were readily available, the birds were bred in increasing numbers. When they moved in swarms, their numbers reached tens of thousands. The sky turned dark and dense with their presence, shrouding the sun in a thick, shifting mass.

The huge flocks of these tiny birds were astounding. Their chirping sounds were like a huge symphony orchestra, and the music they played was earth-shattering. It was the sound of pure nature, which shook the hearts of David and Emily and made them intoxicated.

This kind of bird, like all the other species of birds, has no ambition. It only wants food and drinks, and only wants to reproduce. Apart from that, it has no other aspirations.

Emily: Sometimes I really yearn for the life of these birds, free and carefree.

David: Actually, they are threatened by big birds and snakes. However, their large number makes them to sustain, survive, and reproduce in general.

Emily: Anyway, I think these little birds are a happy bunch. Each year after winter, everything recovers. When spring comes, various birds begin to sing, bringing a warm and prosperous atmosphere. My deepest memory is cuckoo crying.

David: The cuckoo is called "Cuckoo" in the West, "*When You Hear the First. Cuckoo Call in Spring*" is a song by Frederick Delius, a beautiful musical poem. The cuckoo's call is also very popular.

Emily: I remember when I was a child, my friends and I liked to imitate the cuckoo calls. Wc also talked to the cuckoo. Questions and answers used the same tone, for example,

Bugu, Bugu!
Where are you?
I am behind the mountain.
What do you eat?
I eat grasshoppers.
What do you drink?
I drink the dew.

David: Very interesting.
Emily: I hear there is also an indecent side of this bird. Judging from its behavior, it is not a good bird. Cuckoos don't build nests like other birds, but lay their own eggs

in other birds' nests, and let other birds raise their young for them.

David: Some things in the animal kingdom are really incredible. They are not humans after all. They cannot be measured by human thinking.

Emily: In fact, many humans are more cunning and sinister than them.

David: As far as I know, there is another bird called thrush. It is very popular in China.

Emily: Yes. The thrush's cry is very beautiful and pleasant. It is a traditional "cage bird" in China.

David: The fate of cage birds is really sad.

Emily: The bird's greatest fortune lies in its freedom to soar freely in the vast sky. But the "cage bird" is deprived of its freedom.

David: Although the caged bird is favored by people, it turns out to be only the pet and servant of its owner.

David: As far as I know, the Chinese worship a bird "phoenix" which is a combination of gods and birds. It's a bit like the "dragon" of the mythical beast combination.

Emily: The Chinese saying "dragon and phoenix bring prosperity" refers to auspicious and festive events.

David: Phoenix is an immortal bird in Greek mythology. The Nirvana of the Phoenix symbolizes the bird's fiery death and subsequent rebirth from the flames, granting it eternal life. It serves as a metaphor for an indomitable spirit and a relentless will to fight with courage and resilience.

Emily: It seems that the phoenix is a "sacred bird" revered by both the East and the West, although the meaning is different.

David and Emily discovered that the planet Berde was inhabited by a large number of chickens. Although chickens had wings and could fly, they mostly walked on the ground and rarely flew. When the chicken was small, it looked like a pommel ball and chirped, very cute.

David and Emily kept a close eye on the lives of the chickens on the island. In order to make it easier to observe, they lowered their height with the Divine Watch, to be on an equal footing with chickens.

Chickens here lived in groups. They usually foraged around on the grass, laid eggs, and reproduced in the place of residence.

Among the chickens here, there was a leader, who was a big rooster. This chicken was dignified and had extraordinary martial arts skills. David and Emily called him "Ivan". Ivan once fought against the other roosters, and he beat all of them and won the championship, becoming the top chicken ever since. In the flock of chickens, he was overbearing. If he spotted a chicken that displeased him, he would show no mercy— stepping on its back and yanking out its feathers without hesitation.

The chicken that was bullied by him screamed miserably, which was outrageous.

However, the covetous snake in the grass had been defeated by Ivan many times. If there was no Ivan, they would come from time to time and eat eggs and chicks.

Once, Ivan was abusing a hen again. Emily couldn't stand it any longer, she stepped forward to stop the bulling and rescue the hen.

Ivan was furious that he came forward, kicked Emily to the ground, and then stepped on Emily with his strong claws, just like dealing with the hen under his rule.

David adjusted to the mechanism of restoring the prototype of the two on the Divine Watch and shouted for Emily to recite the spell.

After Emily recited the Magic Spell, the two of them suddenly grew taller. Ivan was stunned and became a little bird under the feet of the two of them.

David stepped forward and stepped on Ivan's body. Ivan's neck was stepped on heavily, and he screamed loudly, trying to break free, David's foot stepped harder.

After Ivan calmed down, David released his foot.

Ivan's neck was seriously trampled, and he left bitterly, tilted his head, and limped towards the distance.

Ivan was defeated in this battle, his neck was disabled, and he lost his former glory ever since. His prestige among the flock plummeted. From now on no civilians were bullied by him anymore.

However, the chickens had lost a general to fight against the enemy. The natural enemy of the chicken, the snakes, took advantage of the situation and invaded the territory of the chickens, as if they were invincible, gobbling up chickens and eggs.

David and Emily realized that human intervention in animal herds was not very wise.

One day, as David and Emily were feeding the chickens, they suddenly spotted a few giant birds soaring through the sky, darkening the sun with their massive wings. They hovered for a moment, then swiftly swooped down toward the ground. Two of them caught David and Emily with lightning speed and flew into the sky. Only then did David and Emily realize that these were two giant eagles. David and Emily had always admired the strength and image of eagles, but now they became their prey.

The two were powerless under the firm grip of the giant eagle's claws, unable to use the Divine Watch, and could only wait for the arrangement of their fate. The two were taken to a huge bird's nest by the giant eagle, where several young eagles were waiting to be fed, with their mouths wide open, ready to accept the food brought back by their parents. Two giant eagles relaxed in their home, preparing to tear up their prey and share it piece by piece with the nestlings. Taking advantage of this opportunity, David and Emily used their Divine Watch and Magic Spell and escaped the disaster as fast as lightning.

When the huge eagle family saw their prey, the two of them disappeared without a trace. They looked at each other, but there was nothing they could do.

David and Emily fled back to their original residence, glancing over their shoulders at everything that had just unfolded, still trying to process the chaos that had happened. They were really a little scared. If it weren't for the help of the Divine Watch at the critical moment, the two of them must have become the favorite food of the large eagle family.

The animal kingdom is a natural realm. People's ideas about animals are often subjective or artificial.

In addition, people's views on certain birds are often radically different due to differences in different ethnic groups and regional cultures. This difference in concept has nothing to do with the differences between animals themselves.

For example, the owl is regarded as an unlucky symbol in China, implying death and bad luck. Therefore, it is called an ominous bird, a mourning bird, etc. In

Greece, the owl is a symbol of wisdom, implying wisdom and courage.

The Chinese regard the magpie as a lucky bird, the arrival of the magpie is to report good luck, while the crow is to report bad luck.

In Japan, the crow is considered an auspicious bird, as it is often depicted as a divine messenger in many Japanese fairy tales. Its presence is seen as a symbol of good fortune and spiritual significance.

David and Emily once discussed the animal behavior between them in one of their conversations.

Emily: David, do you think there is any kinship between animals like that between people?

David: Between the spouses of animals, and the relationship between parents and children is sometimes even more intimate than that between humans.

Emily: I once saw a pair of wild geese that got along well day and night. After laying eggs, the female goose sat on the goose eggs all day long. The sun was burning in the sky during the day. It was extremely hot, but the mother insisted on incubating, showing no sign of flinching.

The male goose went out to forage and brought some food to the female goose. It. was just like people's home, with no difference. They gave birth to six young wild geese. The couple took good care of these goslings and looked for food for them. When traveling, the female goose led the goslings to walk in front, and the male goose stretched his neck behind to watch out for any danger. They took good care of the goslings for several months, until the young goslings grew up, could fly to the sky, and then lived independently. The couple had thus completed a natural process and historical mission.

David: It's in the nature of animals to reproduce.

This nature is endowed by God. But that's all. Humans have humanity, ethics, and morality. Animals have none of them.

Emily: So, among animals, and between animals and people, there should be friendship, right? I know that some individual ferocious beasts, such as lions and wolves, because of being brought up since childhood were deeply attached to their human masters. The most common cases are pets such as dogs and cats, they are intimate with people.

David: Humans are a special group of animals. Animals can undergo some adaptive mutations during their close interactions with humans, just as it is reasonable for some wild animals to become domestic. This does not account for a fundamental variation of the whole category of animals.

David and Emily found a bird's egg in the grass. They touched it with their hands and felt some temperature. They concluded that there was a small life growing in it. They didn't know why the bird's egg was abandoned without parental care. They used hay and leaves to make a warm bed for the egg, which was the nest of this little life.

They placed the small bed on a small tree on the slope by the river, with some sunshine during the daytime, thinking it was a safe place and suitable for hatching.

She staggered and couldn't walk steadily after she came out of the shell. Later, she gradually stabilized. David and Emily had been visiting and caring for the little bird every day since then. They liked this little bird very much and named her Lida.

Lida had a good appetite, and she swallowed quickly the food given to her. David and Emily first fed the birds with mollusks, then locusts, and other treats.

Little Lida, the bird, grew stronger each day, her feathers gradually taking on vibrant hues of red, blue, green, and more, becoming a beautiful sight to behold . David and Emily decided it was a beautiful parrot. She was learning to make melodious calls. They began to teach Lida to speak and sing. Lida was smart and eager to learn. She soon learned to say sentences such as "How are you?" "I am fine, thank you." and also to sing songs such as "Happy New Year to you."

One day, when David and Emily came to feed her again, they found that the bird was missing from the nest. And they saw that there were some colorful feathers on the ground under the bird's nest, which obviously belonged to Lida. They immediately felt that something was wrong, and decided that Lida had been assassinated by some wild beast or bird of prey last night. Although they knew that Lida was not very good at flying, they cried out in despair, "Lida! Lida! Where are you?"

David and Emily were devastated by Lida's murder. David couldn't sleep at night, and Emily couldn't sleep and eat well.

After quite some time, Lida's murder gradually faded away. David and Emily felt that such things were commonplace in the animal world, so they had to live with it internally.

One day while David and Emily were walking on the prairie, suddenly a beautiful bird flew from the nearby dense forest. It seemed to be a parrot, but it was very big, like a pigeon. It was a big parrot that had never been seen on Earth. Like an old friend, this big parrot flew directly to the shoulders of David and Emily, and even talked to them, greeting them "How are you?" David and Emily were very happy. Lida didn't die, she was still alive and well.

Later, David and Emily saw the colorful feather residues on the paw of a dead bird of prey. They guessed that Lida was attacked by a bird of prey that night. Lida avoided the bird of prey skillfully and survived the death, thus they reunited with their old friend today.

Emily: Birds are an interesting category of animals. Most birds can move in the air and on land, have wings that can fly with, and some can move in water, both flying and swimming, like geese and ducks. So, birds have more freedom. Unlike fish, which are limited by water. Terrestrial animals are limited by land.

David: There is also a category of birds that do not fly. In addition to chickens that usually don't fly, there are also ostriches and penguins. Their wings are useless and they usually walk on two legs. Ostriches run very fast and are known to be good runners.

Emily: It is said that the ancestors of ostriches and penguins are dinosaurs. Is it right?

David: This statement is not groundless. It has a basis. This is the change that dinosaurs were forced to adapt to the new environment before extinction.

Emily: I think it's at least a reasonable speculation.

David: In addition to the non-existent god bird Phoenix, among the birds, the first is the eagle. Eagle worship has ancient roots, present in many cultures. Whether among the Manchu, Mongol, Kazak peoples, or in the Roman Empire, the eagle was revered as a symbol of divinity and strength. The German Nazi Party during World War II was known as the Nazi Eagle.

Emily: The centerpiece of the national emblem of the United States of America is a bald eagle. The eagle is the national bird of the United States and is the symbol of strength, courage, freedom, and immortality.

David: The image of the eagle is extremely majestic and brave. A well-deserved symbol of America.

Emily: I agree. I found that people's views on birds were often somewhat romantic, mostly out of people's subjective consciousness. The bird world is much more complicated than people think. In human literary works, birds in the sky are always regarded as a beautiful background, a foil to the picture, and a poetic description. In fact, these ideas only exist in people's minds. It exists in the author's own will and the resonance of readers.

David: Yes. I agree with you, Emily.

On a sunny morning, David and Emily were collecting wild berries on the prairie, and couldn't help singing a cheerful song. The singing was gentle and melodious.

Emily sang the beautiful tune of *Scarborough Fair*.

Are you going to the Scarborough Fair?
Parsley, sage, rosemary, and thyme
Please give my regards to a girl there
She used to be my true love.

David sang the wild song "*Live*".

You're stayin' alive stayin' alive
Feel the city breakin'
Ah ha ha ha stayin' alive stayin'
alive Ah ha ha ha stayin' alive

The singing of the two first attracted the parrot Lida in the forest. Lida then sang loudly, with a high-pitched and gorgeous voice. Later, countless different kinds of chaffinches were attracted to join the chorus, chirping and chattering, so lively.

This shocking chorus also mobilized all kinds of insects on the grassland to express the joy in their hearts together. Hundreds of cicadas were vocalizing together on the tree, chile, chi-le! Grasshoppers on the grass vibrated their wings and made a clucking sound.

The species in the water were not willing to lag behind, and a large number of frogs were shouting together at the water's edge. The underwater dolphins and seals emerged from the water to make their sounds, with thick and high-pitched voices.

It was a truly spectacular scene, showcasing a magnificent gathering as creatures from the water, land, and air came together, their voices blending in an indulgent chorus of nature's harmony.

David and Emily's heart was agitated, and all this made them unforgettable for the rest of their lives.

Emily: David, look at the swans in the sky. This reminds me of the beautiful ballet of "Swan Lake".

Emily couldn't help humming the wonderful music of Swan Lake, the masterpiece of Tchaikovsky's genius. The two were intoxicated in the enjoyment of the beautiful melody and light dance steps.

At the same time, they watched the white swans in the sky, their beautiful images. They were dancing to the beautiful melody of music.

At this incomparable beautiful moment, all the swans acted in unison and each took a puddle of shit at the command of the swan leader. The swan feces that fell from the sky fluttered and scattered, like a meteorite rain, which was spectacular.

David and Emily's beautiful feelings for the swans suddenly faded. The two of them smiled knowingly, because they were familiar with nature and the animal kingdom. Nature doesn't always pander to people's romantic feelings.

Chapter 6

THE HUMAN WORLD

So far, David and Emily had traveled to five planets in the Silver Way Galaxy of Universe B and had seen five different worlds: Dinosaur, Jungle, Insect, Water, and Bird. These planets were *unmanned worlds* when they first arrived.

This time, David and Emily planned to switch to a different galaxy. They searched on the Divine Watch and found that there was a Golden Way System in Universe B, where there was a hot star like the sun, surrounded by hundreds of planets of various sizes. David and Emily named this star the Red Sun and this galaxy the Red Sun System. The Red Sun System was much larger than the solar system in the Milky Way System in Universe Λ.

At the same time, David and Emily discovered that there were multiple human-inhabited planets in the Red Sun System. After exploring various organisms on unmanned planets, they planned to explore and experience human life in another universe, and conduct a comparative study with humans on Earth. They thought it would be very meaningful and interesting.

In the vast Red Sun System, David and Emily first arrived at a planet known as Humin, where modern humans lived.

The temperature on Humin Star was suitable for human life. Due to the thicker atmosphere on this star, the temperature difference between different regions on the planet was much smaller than that on Earth, and there was basically no clear distinction between tropical, temperate, and frigid zones.

A large number of people lived on this planet. Their appearance was different from that of human beings on Earth. People's skin was slightly reddish, whether this was caused by the Red Sun of the Red Sun System was still unknown.

These people were no less civilized than the Earth people. They had culture and education systems similar to those of the people on Earth.

The country where David and Emily lived was called Natu. Natu Country was the largest and most developed country on Humin.

The language spoken by the people in this country was different from the human languages on Earth with its own unique pronunciation, grammar, and vocabulary. David and Emily were gradually learning and mastering them, and gradually communicating with the local people.

On this planet, as on Earth, humans were absolutely dominant. Humans would always be number one in the biota. There were many kinds of creatures on the planet, including birds, beasts, bees, butterflies, fish, and insects, all over the water, land, and air. These creatures were subservient to humans who were second to none.

The people here believed that the reason why humans could occupy a superior position in nature and possess extraordinary abilities was mainly due to their superb wisdom and knowledge. Here, humans placed great value on culture and education, honoring those with knowledge and wisdom as pillars of society.

Natu National Academy of Sciences was the highest academic institution in the country. It played a crucial role in the development and strength of the country. Its status in people's minds was not below the government of the country.

David and Emily found a research job at the institute, and their research project was anthropology.

Natu National Academy of Sciences was headed by the Dean Mr. Charp. Mr. Charp was an academic leader in several disciplines. He not only achieved significant research results and wrote numerous books, but also was upright and fair in handling affairs. He was enthusiastic toward people, had an outgoing personality, and had a good sense of humor.

Mr. Charp was bald, no hair on his head, showing abnormal brightness. He said that he overworked his brain and exhausted all the hair on his head.

Under the overall arrangement of the Science Research Academy, David's research topic was *"The Variation of Animal Morphology in Historical Evolution The Role of External Factors"*. Emily's research topic was *"Human Relationships with Other Living Creatures History and Current Situation"*.

Because they had gained rich experience and accumulated a lot of first-hand information in their interstellar travel, they had made breakthroughs in the academic field and achieved fruitful results, which were widely recognized and praised by the academic community of the country.

Mr. Charp highly appreciated David and Emily's academic research achievements and viewpoints. He often remarked that among his colleagues in the Academy of Sciences, David and Emily—the two young visitors from outer space—had brought fresh energy and new perspectives to their institution. He said that if David and Emily had come a few years earlier, the hair on his head would not have all fallen out.

Mr. Charp enjoyed discussing knowledge and exchanging ideas with David and Emily. He particularly praised David and Emily for their inquisitive and thoughtful spirit. Some of his research methods also gave David and Emily useful inspiration. Mr. Charp said that when starting to think about a major issue, one should keep the mind as calm as the calm water, and use rigorous logical reasoning to thread through a large amount of factual materials. Often, inspiration would come at this time, and reasonable deductions would be obtained. This was the moment when the waves were magnificent.

In addition, David and Emily believed that although human beings had absolute dominance in the biological world, humans should treat other creatures well, including animals and plants, and live in harmony with nature.

David and Emily found that there were some stray dogs and cats there. At first, they took some food to them every day. Then they adopted two dogs, Adams and Stephanie, and two cats, Jack and Laurel. The dogs and cats they adopted were nurtured with great care and grew so close to them that they became like family. The dogs slept on the floor of their bedroom at night. The cats slept on the sofa, sometimes on their bed.

David and Emily knew very well that the relationship between humans and animals was gradually created by mutual trust and influence.

People here were very positive about David and Emily's practice of taking in stray dogs and cats.

At the same time, the stories of them traveling from another universe by the artifact were also being spread among the people.

People here were full of curiosity about their artifacts. Most people only knew that their auras were omnipotent and could make them go wherever they wanted, the destination could be near or far. At the same time, the Divine Watch could also make them smaller and bigger. David and Emily were living in a new human environment. They worked conscientiously and got along well with their colleagues. Among their colleagues, there was a senior academician named Phiss, who had a close relationship with them and they had become good friends. He often introduced David and Emily to various features in the local area and in the Academy, so that they could adapt to everything here as soon as possible. David and Emily were naturally very grateful to Mr. Phiss.

As a local resident, Mr. Phiss enthusiastically introduced local attractions to David and Emily, and also took them to go shopping, sightseeing, playing ball games, swimming and watching movies.

One day, Mr. Phiss took David and Emily to a scenic spot called Ghost Valley.

There was a trestle bridge at the top of Ghost Valley.

Phiss: People here say that whoever can walk to the end of this trestle bridge is a brave man. A brave man is highly respected in this country.

David: Can I have a try? Phiss: Of course.

Emily: No, David. That bridge is not strong, it is too dangerous.

Phiss: Let me go first and show you.

He walked on the bridge for a while, and then returned.

David: It's my turn.

David then walked onto the bridge. After walking for a while, the bridge began to shake, and then they heard the sound of cracking, the bridge deck began to break.

Seeing the situation, David skillfully jumped to the side of the deep valley and grabbed an exposed root on the valley wall. Unexpectedly, the root was not strong enough and broke after a while. David slipped down the steep valley. When Emily saw this, she shouted, "David! David!" and then rolled down the slope of the valley.

Phiss yelled, "Emily, don't go down, it's an abyss. It's dangerous!"

Emily no longer cared about the danger. When she was in danger in the Rocky Mountains and fell from the mountain about a decade ago, it was David who rolled down the hillside to save her.

Indeed, the abyss was quite deep. David and Emily rolled down the slope and were blocked by a piece of protruding rock on the slope. The two were hanging on the valley slope. Although they were wounded in multiple places, they survived. If they continued to fall, the two of them would surely perish.

David and Emily were hanging on the side of the ravine at this time, unable to reach the sky or descend to the ground. If it was on the hillside, they could be rescued by a helicopter, but the helicopter could not fly into the abyss where they were now.

In this situation, they naturally thought of their Watch and Spell.

David struggled painfully, took out the watch, and set the position on it to return to the ground at the top of the valley. After that Emily issued an order, and the two returned to the ground where they were before they fell.

Seeing the two of them returning from the deep valley, Phiss said, "I told you that the trestle bridge was too dangerous. Fortunately, the wonderful watch saved you."

Phiss seemed very attentive and quickly found a car to take the two of them to the hospital.

David: Thank you!

After this incident, Emily began to be aware that there was something unusual about Phiss.

Emily: David, don't you think it's a bit of a coincidence that we nearly lost our lives in Ghost Valley last time? I think it was Phiss who brought us into danger.

David: Phiss is warm and friendly to us and helped us a lot. Let's not think ill of others. We should trust each other with our colleagues.

Emily: The relationship between humans is complex.

David and Emily made outstanding achievements in academic research, and they were awarded the title of meritorious academicians. This great honor was enviable.

Coupled with the wonderful artifact, the two had become well-known celebrities in the Natu Kingdom, on Humin planet.

Once, Phiss proposed to David and Emily to perform their magic skills in front of the public. David and Emily said that they usually used their Divine Watch in special cases or critical moments. However, Phiss and a few others persisted, urging them repeatedly. Finding the hospitality difficult to refuse, David and Emily reluctantly agreed—but only to demonstrate the changes in their height and figure without moving from their place.

David began to adjust the knob on the Divine Watch, after that, Emily immediately chanted the Magic Spell. Under the eyes of everyone, the two suddenly became as big as dogs and cats. This caused a round of applause from the crowd. Someone in the audience shouted, "Can you guys be still smaller?" After a little adjustment, David and Emily became as small as beetles. The audience looked carefully at the ground, and some people could not even see such small persons there. When David and Emily returned to their original shape, that was, their original height, they adjusted and chanted again. This time the two became as tall as giraffes. It drew warm applause. Someone in the audience shouted, "Can you guys go even taller?" After a little adjustment, David and Emily became as tall as the church bell tower. The audience cheered again enthusiastically.

Since then, David and Emily become famous in this country. Their friend Phiss congratulated them.

Shortly after that, a tragedy happened in the city. Mr. Charp, the president of the Science Research Academy, died suddenly and lay dead on the street. It looked like he fell from a height. There were no high-rise buildings in this city except the bell tower of the church. And Mr. Charp's body was not near the bell tower.

There were a lot of discussions among the residents, and some people began to suspect David and Emily, saying that they fell Mr. Charp from a height after becoming taller with their Divine Watch, and caused the tragedy. David and Emily refuted this accusation, saying they had no motive for committing the crime. Mr. Charp had always supported them academically. Under his strong recommendation, David and Emily were awarded meritorious academicians. Mr. Charp's death had nothing to do with them.

When the police came to the scene for investigations, they concluded that Mr. Charp fell from a certain height and died.

David and Emily were the biggest suspects in this case, because they were the only ones in the country who could take Mr. Charp to that height. David and Emily were taken to the police station for detention and interrogation. In order to prevent them from escaping with the Divine Watch, the amulet was temporarily held, and the two were detained separately.

Before David and Emily were taken away by the police, they asked the police to help take care of their dogs and cats after they left and said that these dogs and cats were very smart and might help them solve cases. At that time, the police did not have their own police dogs, so they agreed to give it a try.

The people in the city, inspired by some people, like Phiss, set off a wave of *"anti-monsters"*. They said that David and Emily killed their technology giant and blocked their technological progress. The two people had harmed the people with witchcraft and had done endless damage to the country.

They said that the two criminals should be burned at the stake.

In this grim situation, David and Emily were under great pressure. Since the amulet was detained by the police, their hope of escaping with the amulet had also been shattered.

David and Emily spent their days in prison. They had nothing to do with the murder case, but they were accused as murderers for no reason, and were blamed and held accountable by local residents of Humin Star. Both of them were suffering physically and mentally. However, they did not regret the trip. They had long been mentally prepared for the difficulties and bumps encountered on their journey.

After a period of time, the case suddenly took a turn for the better. The dogs, Adams and Stephanie, and the cats, Jack and Laura, adopted by David and Emily, had undergone rigorous training at the police station. Their keen senses and intelligence made them valuable assets in solving cases, assisting officers with tracking, detection, and even uncovering hidden clues. Adam and Stephanie dug up some traces of human blood on a flat ground at the foot of the bell tower. Jack and Laura pulled out a bloody handkerchief from a nearby drain. According to police identification, the bell tower was the scene of the murder. Charp was killed when he fell from the top of the bell tower. According to the evidence obtained at the scene, this case might be a homicide, someone deliberately murdered Mr. Charp.

So, who was the murderer?

The bloody handkerchief recovered from the drain spoke for itself. It was identified that this handkerchief belonged to Academician Phiss, and there was not only Mr. Charp's blood on it, but also the DNA of Academician Phiss.

An elderly man living nearby reported the incident to the police, saying that on the evening of the crime he had seen Mr. Charp, accompanied by Academician Phiss, climbed to the top of the bell tower of the church. Mr. Charp might have fallen from the building and died.

The investigators of the case investigated Academician Phiss. Phiss' bloody handkerchief was issued. In the face of ironclad evidence Academician Phiss admitted that he accompanied President Charp up to the bell tower that day in order to observe the meteor shower that night from a high place. He said President Charp died by accidentally falling from the top tier of the building.

David and Emily were released from the suspicion of murdering President Charp.

During this period, it was revealed that Academician Phiss did not report the case in time after the incident, but instead spread rumors to slander David and Emily among the crowd, confused people, and set off public opinion to execute David and Emily.

The investigators of the case concentrated the suspect in the case on Academician Phiss. After some in-depth investigation, with the bloody handkerchief as the evidence Academician Phiss had to confess his crime. He was the one who pushed President Charp off the top of the bell tower that night. In order to deceive people, he took advantage of the dead of night and dragged the body of President Charp from under the bell tower to an open field in the distance. The open area was where David and Emily performed the magic power of their watch and spell in public. He also buried the blood under the bell tower with dirt to create the illusion that Mr. Charp did not die of falling from the bell tower.

The prime culprit who killed President Charp turned out to be Academician Phiss. Previously, he had tried to kill David and obtain the Divine Watch but failed.

Later, after careful planning, he killed President Charp. The plan was to succeed the President of the Science Academy after the death of the President, and at the same time, to blame David and Emily for the murder, so as to eliminate his competitors by the way. This was his wishful thinking.

This case shocked David and Emily. It was unexpected that their best friend, Academician Phiss, would have killed President Charp behind their backs, and insidiously accused them both. Human beings were more sinister than other animals. David and Emily's experience in Humin's human world inevitably chilled them after traveling to several animal-dominated worlds, they had thought that the human world would have given them more care and warmth, but that was not the case.

On the contrary, the dogs and cats adopted by them were sincere to them, helping them escape when they were in danger.

Nevertheless, David and Emily still believed that humans were a fully developed, intelligent animal group that was moving towards a higher level of civilization. The lack of humanity and rationality in some people could not change the superior position of human beings in the universe and the world. There were still many kind and righteous people like Mr. Charp in human beings.

David and Emily not only had a profound influence in Natu Country, Humin Planet, but also gained popularity in the local society. They found that the music here was very unrestrained and lyrical. At the same time, at the request of the young people here, David and Emily also taught them to sing beautiful songs on the Earth, such as *"Auld Lang Syne"* and *"My Heart Will Eternal"* and so on.

Because David and Emily looked younger after they came to the new universe, they were regarded as handsome young men and beautiful girls by the local people.

With frequent contact, the relationship of David and Emily with the local people had become increasingly close.

A man, Soochi fell in love with Emily and proposed to her many times, which was declined by Emily politely.

A girl named Hena fell in love with David. She frankly expressed her love for

David. David told her that his heart had been given to Emily and politely declined Vera's courtship. However, Hena did not stop there and still had a special liking for David. She not only regarded David as a mysterious "*alien*", but also believed that David was a perfect "*divine man*" or "*god*". She openly expressed her love for David to Emily. Hena believed that David had a perfect personality, rich knowledge and experiences, strong will and sympathy for the weak, and so on. Hena hoped to share with Emily her love for David and David's love for the opposite gender.

Emily recalled that when David traveled alone to East Africa a million years ago, he brought back a woman named Nava who loved him deeply. The three of them had been close together for a period of time, and then Nava passed away. Emily still remembered that wonderful time. Emily told Hena that she fully understood Hena's love for David. She said she would convey Hena's wishes to David.

David had a deep talk with Hena. He expressed his understanding and gratitude to Hena for her love and patiently explained to Hena why this matter was difficult to achieve. David said he and Emily were just passing through here. The two of them came from another universe, traveling between several planets, and would leave here soon. Their journey was completely dependent on the Divine Watch and Magic Spell. Since the power of the amulet could only affect the two holders, they could not take Hena with them when they left. So, he hoped that Hena could understand the difficulty. Hena expressed her understanding but asked whether David and Emily could stay and not leave. David and Emily said that they still had a family and relatives on a planet called Earth in another universe, and they were looking forward to their return soon.

Hena felt pretty lost, and her eyes were filled with sparkling tears.

David and Emily were ready to end their trip to the star Humin and go to another planet. Many people here hoped to retain the two of them. In particular, the colleagues of the Science Research Academy earnestly requested that they should stay here and continue their work. David and Emily were honored by the proposal of a promotion and salary increase, along with the recommendation to become academic leaders. However, they politely declined, expressing their gratitude while emphasizing that their pursuit was knowledge and exploration rather than titles or material rewards.

The dogs and cats adopted by David and Emily naturally did not want them to leave. They handed over these dogs and cats to the police and allowed them to assist in solving cases when necessary. The police readily accepted.

David and Emily embarked on a new journey of their interstellar roaming.

Chapter 7

THE GLUTTONOUS WORLD

avid and Emily arrived at the planet Glute in the Red Sun System of Universe B.

There were three main countries on this planet. In addition to the "Vicca" where they now lived, there were also "Watowa" and "Tilews". Among these three countries, Watowa had the largest territory and the strongest national power. Vicca State was the smallest.

The common feature of these three countries was that basic human desires were fully developed and indulged. It was believed that satisfying people's basic desires was the highest happiness index of the people here.

Although these people had various skin colors, they were mostly full of joy. They thought they lived in a happy era and a pleasant country. Enthusiastic locals arranged accommodations for David and Emily.

They soon integrated into the society of the planet.

People on this planet placed great importance on diet, believing that food was the foundation of life. The saying *"food is the paramount necessity for people"* was widely recognized, emphasizing the central role of nourishment in their daily lives and culture. The people on Glute believed that the first priority of human beings was to eat and drink well. Eating and drinking well was the goal and great ideal of all people, the symbol of social progress and the key to cultural development.

Among the fundamental necessities of life—food, clothing, housing, and transportation—food was given the highest priority. Streets were lined with various establishments catering to this need, including food stores, cooked food shops, non-staple food markets, restaurants, pubs, cafés, and teahouses, each offering a diverse array of culinary delights. The food streets were full of various food stalls. The food stalls displayed a wide variety of cooked and semi-cooked foods such as meat, seafood, and vegetarian food. The shoppers drool over the delicious delicacies. Many customers were sitting by the stall to eat.

Dining culture has been brought to the extreme on this planet. There was a food processing department in the universities, which was divided into cooking and seasoning majors, beverage and wine majors, etc. Students could study for bachelor's, master's, and doctoral degrees in food processing. All kinds of chefs with good knowledge and skills were respected by people.

Catering had become the country's primary industry. Related industries, such as food processing, pig raising, sheep raising, chicken raising, duck raising, fishing, etc., were very prosperous. It had driven the economy of the whole country. The food processing industry also drove agriculture, animal husbandry, and marine fishing. The economy of Vicca was thriving.

It was said that the other two countries, Watowa and Tilews, had similar or even more serious situations. Their pursuit of food taste was even more than that of Vicca.

In the state of Tilews, people became addicted to alcohol, and taverns and bars flourished everywhere. Various beverages, especially alcoholic beverages, were on the market and were available in large quantities. People's taste in fine wine was getting higher and more professional. There are also professional bartenders and tasters. The professional level of bartenders and tasters was no less than that of industry experts on Earth.

One could see people enjoying delicious food and wine everywhere. Many people were eating and drinking in restaurants and bars. There were also professional singers singing alongside and professional pianists playing music. It looked like a scene of singing and dancing. Of course, some people got drunk to the fullest, while others were so drunk that they yelled and played like crazy.

People who drank heavily were revered. Excessive advocates of food and wine were not considered *gluttonous*, but were regarded as natural and unrestrained.

The liquor and beverage specialty stores in Tilews were highly developed, which led to the development of the brewing industry and other beverage industries, as well as the revitalization of agriculture and the wine tableware industry.

The Tilews Kingdom had both the economic characteristics and strength of the service industry of Vicca State and Watowa Kingdom. It occupied a superposition in the alcohol industry, especially the beverage industry, and had an overwhelming advantage over the other two countries. The Watowa Kingdom vigorously advocated meat eating, claiming that mcat could strengthen people's physical fitness and enhance the combat effectiveness of the army.

Wagigi, the king of Watowa Kingdom, was a licentious and immoral tyrant. He regarded himself as the king of a great country, and its national strength was strong, so he acted recklessly. He was lustful, gluttonous, and drunk to the point of heinous.

He not only had a strong desire for sex and appetite but also had a lust for power, attempting to possess the supreme power of the country, the world, and even all mankind.

He had three queens and one hundred concubines. There was also a beauty pageant to choose beauties from the folks every year, to replace unsatisfactory concubines or simply to taste *fresh flesh*.

King Wagigi had the world's most brilliant chef to prepare three meals for him every day. In addition to delicacies from mountains and seas, there were all famous dishes and delicacies in the world. In addition to the meat of all kinds of domestic animals, he was also keen on tasting all kinds of game, such as wild buffalo, wild boar, wild sheep, rabbits, wild geese, wild ducks, pheasants, and so on from the sky, and fresh fish, turtles, shrimps, crabs, and so on from the water.

The most incredible thing was that King Wagigi was ingenious, combining beautiful women, delicacies, and fine wines. He ordered the court chef to cook him a rare delicacy— "Three-Beauty Feast". This dish "Three-Beauty Feast" included human flesh—the flesh of beautiful women. King Wagigi decided that the meat of a beautiful woman was delicious, accompanied by other delicious ingredients and fine wine. It would be the most beautiful taste enjoyment in the world.

According to the laws of Watowa Kingdom, people had the right to eat human meat and human meat products in addition to animal meat products. That was to say, in addition to animal meat, cannibalism was also allowed. Human flesh was the top grade in food. Dishes and food processed with human flesh were expensive, and most of them were luxuries enjoyed by high-ranking officials.

Human meat dishes were an essential part of the daily diet of the king and dignitaries of Watowa. The sources of human flesh were mainly prison inmates and prisoners of war. Sometimes also from kidnapping civilians. Some young and middle-aged men and women among the common people were neither fat nor thin. If they were selected as superior ingredients, they might be hunted and killed for meat to cook as delicacies.

The greatest joy of Wagigi, king of Watowa Kingdom, was to choose beauties among the people, which were called "Beauty Dedicated to the King". Beauty Dedicated to the King was sent to the royal palace for the king to enjoy. After using it, the beauties were killed, and the meat was cooked as a delicacy, accompanied by fine wine, claiming that this was the full enjoyment of *beauty*.

The king of Vicca State, Welson, was a young, promising and enlightened monarch. Under his leadership, Vicca State implemented a series of reform bills that restricted royal power and benefited people's livelihood and civil rights. At the same time, in the new policy, there were also provisions limiting excessive indulgence. The king set an example by having no concubines except for one queen. And it clearly stipulated that the consumption of human flesh was prohibited in Vicca State.

King Welson had several conversations with David and Emily. He was interested in how humans lived in another universe. Emily introduced the *"Seven Emotions and Six Desires"* of human beings to the king. Seven Emotions: Joy, Anger, Sadness, Thinking, Sadness, Fear, Shock. Six Desires: Appetite, Sexual Desire, Lust, Possessive Desire, Desire for Knowledge, Desire to Excel.

King Welson: I agree very much with the view that people have Seven Emotions and Six Desires. These emotions are the natural expression of people's mentality in different situations, otherwise they would be insensitive to everything, being tantamount to vegetables. From a positive perspective, human desires are the driving force for people's lives and progress. Without this pursuit, life will lose its meaning.

David: Your Majesty is quite right. There should be appropriate control over human desires. Excessive tolerance and indulgence of various desires will inevitably lead to negative consequences.

King Wilson: I have long recognized this issue.

Today, I am taking the opportunity to talk with you, the two distant sages with humble hearts, asking you to introduce the good strategies of another country in the other universe to deal with human desires, in order to serve as a reference for our governance.

Emily: Your Majesty need not be humble. We are from the planet of Earth of another universe. Each of the more than 200 countries on the Earth has its own national policies, laws, and customs. Possessiveness, thirst for knowledge, and desire to excel are mostly encouraged there. Natural appetite, sexual desire, etc. should not be restrained.

But its excessive indulgence should not be advocated and indulged.

David: I believe that excessive indulgence would inevitably lead to the degeneration of human nature, the increase of crime rate, and the breeding of parasites and black sheep in society, such as sluggards, hooligans, thieves, and local ruffians.

King Welson: Quite right. I agree with your opinion.

King Welson won the hearts of the people for his foresight and insight. People had realized that the reform of Vicca State was beneficial to the country's prosperity and the people's strength, and was moving towards a higher stage of human civilization.

The new policy currently being implemented by the Vicca State made the Vicca State's economy prosperous and its national strength reinforced.

David and Emily each found their own jobs in Vicca. David conducted biological research with fellow biologists here and worked at a research facility. Emily shared her experience with her fellow artists here and engaged in artistic discussion and creation in an art salon every day.

Young people in the new world were full of passion, striving to make progress, invincible, and infinitely creative. They were determined to break new ground and usher in a bright future for mankind.

David and Emily quickly integrated into the ordinary people here. Although they spoke completely different languages, they seemed to share a common voice and understand each other to a greater extent.

People here were friendly and sincere. David and Emily soon made some friends in Vicca State.

David and Emily discussed some issues about life outlook in their conversations with local friends.

David and Emily asked whether there should be a noble purpose in life. On the issue of diet, people still had quite different opinions on the basic question of *"live to eat"* or *"eat to live."*

Many people on this planet were passionate about delicious food, believing that by eating poorly, life would be meaningless. Full enjoyment of delicious food was a tangible happiness and joy.

Others suggested that eating was to live and that humans should have more important pursuits and goals. If one only pursued good food and drink, what was the difference from ordinary animals? Human beings were advanced creatures and should take on more important missions.

Many young people in the country of Vicca had begun to take a critical attitude towards the severe gluttony and tradition on Glute.

David and Emily learned the local language and songs from local young people. The political reform of Vicca State had been widely supported by the people in the country.

The King of the Watowa Kingdom believed that this reform threatened his rule and hated the reform of Vicca State to death.

Wagigi, the king of the Watowa Kingdom, launched a large-scale military campaign against the Vicca State. He attempted to conquer Vicca State and promote his extremely indulgent ideology to the outside world. On the other hand, he tried to use this to shock domestic dissidents and suppress domestic anti-royal trends.

Facing the crisis of a mighty army pressing down on the border, under the leadership of King Welson, Vicca State rose up to meet the enemy. However, due to the outnumbered enemies, the War of Resistance was somewhat tight. Wagigi's army had occupied most of the land of Vicca State, and Vicca State was in danger.

At the time of national crisis, David joined the army and the struggle against the invaders. He fought bravely with his comrades in the army and made repeated military achievements. In a battle, David's army was surrounded by the enemy. After running out of ammunition and food, he and several of his comrades tried to break through and were captured by the enemy. They were imprisoned in a dark room, waiting to be taken to the enemy country for slaughter, which was their inevitable fate. Their meat would also be cut off as cooking ingredients, such as cattle, sheep, and pigs.

Emily stayed in the rear, engaged in logistics and caring for the sick and wounded. When she learned the news that David had been captured by the Watowa army, she was extremely anxious.

To make matters worse, the Watowa army intended to capture beautiful women in the enemy country as the best offering to King Wagigi. One day, while Emily was cooking for the wounded, several soldiers of the enemy rushed in. They were the special police team of Watowa Kingdom, and they specialized in finding "Beauty Dedicated to the King" for the king. They took a fancy to Emily at once, and then took her away and transported her to King Wagigi's Palace.

Thinking of David's inevitable fate of being slaughtered by the enemy, Emily racked her brains and tried to escape from the dilemma with David. She and David were usually together. They could use the Divine Watch and Magic Spell to transform together and escape from danger. Now that they were not together, this magic was difficult to execute. David in trouble also thought of this magic way, but he and Emily were in different places now. What should they do?

During this period, Princess Seshasha of Tilews was on a friendly tour in Vicca State. Unfortunately, the Watowa army invaded Vicca State. The special police team of Watowa Kingdom arrested Princess Seshasha in the operation of looking for the "Beauty Dedicated to the King" and quickly transported them to the palace of Watowa Kingdom. Princess Seshasha was young and especially beautiful. This made King Wagigi excited and joyful. He congratulated himself for his luckiness.

When Nitoto, king of the Tilews Kingdom, learned of this, he was furious.

He demanded that Watowa Kingdom immediately return the princess. Wagigi, the king of Watowa Kingdom, insisted not to follow.

Firstly, his power was at its peak, and it would soon conquer Vicca State. Secondly, he had a rare princess in his grasp, reveling in his fortune—a beautiful concubine at his side and a feast before him. How could he be willing to spit out the delicious food from his mouth?

The Tilews Kingdom immediately declared war on the Watowa Kingdom and fought side by side with the Vicca State to fight the war of aggression against the Watowa. So, the war situation had improved significantly. The army of Watowa was losing ground. The joined forces of Vicca State and Tilews Kingdom launched a massive counterattack.

In the royal palace of Watowa, Emily met Seshasha, the princess of Tilews who was abducted to the palace of Watowa. Princess Seshasha asked about Emily's origin. When she learned that Emily was from Vicca State, she told Emily about her miserable situation, saying that she was in danger of being insulted, executed, and eating meat at any time.

Emily was deeply moved by the princess's tragic fate and gently inquired about the king's daily life and routines. Princess Seshasha, understanding the gravity of the situation, agreed to cooperate with Emily, determined to free herself from the king's grasp. The two made a plan to let Princess Seshasha add some mongoose to the king's drink. The princess acted according to the plan. The mongoose worked as expected. After drinking the beverage, the king was bedridden and kept in a coma.

The Watowa Kingdom was leaderless and the senior military and political officials were in a mess. Emily took the opportunity to escape with Princess Seshasha. On the way to escape, the two disguised themselves as civilians of Watowa. They were taken in by a kind-hearted wife of a cattle farm and lived in the owner's house.

David, who was held in the prison camp of the Watowa army, was trying to escape at this time. He adjusted on the Watch and found the place to escape, but couldn't start it because Emily was not there. Suddenly he noticed that the Divine Watch was trembling, and he thought that it might be Emily who was in a different place, reciting the spell silently. David couldn't help but say, "That's great, Emily." In this way, the Divine Watch was activated, and David and Emily came from different places to the place David had selected on the Divine Watch at the same time. The reunion of the two after a long separation naturally excited them immensely. After not seeing each other for many days, the two suddenly reunited and embraced warmly.

Emily informed David about the situation of Princess Seshasha. They found the cattle farm where Emily and Princess Seshasha took refuge in the oracle. The two accompanied the princess back to the kingdom of Tilews. Princess Seshasha was very grateful.

On the way to Tilews with Princess Seshasha, David and Emily met some troops of Watowa. When those soldiers learned that Princess Seshasha was at large, they naturally couldn't bear it. They wanted to capture the princess and send her back to King Wagigi in the palace of Watowa.

David and Emily used their artifacts to enlarge their bodies and fought against the Watowa troops. After several rounds, the Watowa troops were defeated. The three continued to march towards the country of Tilews.

Nitoto, king of Tilews, was very excited when he saw his daughter Seshasha return safely after being in distress. Princess Seshasha talked to her father about David and Emily's life-saving grace. King Nitoto was very grateful to them.

King Nitoto kept David and Emily in the palace and treated them as VIPs every day.

The king even proposed to betroth Princess Seshasha to David, saying that this was the wish of the princess herself. David said he was married and would not marry again. The king said that Emily could find another new love, and Prince Wakuku had already fallen in love with Emily. If both marriages were successful, it would be a double happiness.

David and Emily had a hard time accepting this. The two repeatedly evaded, saying that both of them were middle-aged and had passed the appropriate age for marriage. The king said that was the age of the other universe. In this place, they were still young. He also said that the princess and the prince insisted on this marriage, and their wishes were hard to resist.

David and Emily were so helpless that they had to escape with the help of the Divine

Watch. The two returned to their preferred country of Vicca.

At this time, the allied forces of Tilews and Vicca launched a major counter-offensive, which was overwhelming and they had already occupied most of Watowa's territory. One of the major missions of the Tilews army was to rescue Princess Seshasha. Due to poor communication devices at that time, the Tilews army didn't know that Princess Seshasha had already returned to the country of Tilews. After the army captured the Watowa Palace, they searched the palace extensively, but did not find Princess Saishasha, thinking that the princess had been killed. In a rage, they killed King Wagigi, who was already unconscious. Watowa had no leader, and the country was in chaos.

The remnants of the army bowed their knees and surrendered.

The Watowa Kingdom was defeated, and in the aftermath of the war, the once brutal regime was dismantled. Under the supervision of Vicca State and Tilews Kingdom, Watowa abolished its totalitarian and cannibalistic policies, replacing them with a new state system that emphasized humanity, justice, and compassion.

Chapter 8

The Demon World

fter David and Emily left Glute Star, they came to Demon Star.

There were more than one hundred countries, large and small, on this planet.

David and Emily's foothold was in a larger country called the Five-Thorn Kingdom on the planet.

This country did not look much different from other countries they had roamed so far. The citizens here were all working hard to make a living.

David and Emily gradually learned some local languages in their contacts.

After people here learned about the origins of David and Emily, they found it unbelievable that these two people were actually from another universe! The locals respected David and Emily as divine beings.

David and Emily associated with the people here and made some good friends. Among them were Mr. Charge, Mr. Hallef, and Ms. Merlin.

In talking with people here, David and Emily learned that this was an abnormal country. It was not the ordinary people here who were abnormal, but the politicians who controlled the country were a bunch of monsters. This group of demons and ghosts had seized high administrative positions within the kingdom, wielding their power to bring harm and suffering to the people, perpetuating fear and cruelty throughout the land. They were actually ferocious, red-haired, and green-faced, killing people without blinking an eye, but wearing beautiful painted skins, pretending to be harmless, and fooling the common people.

They claimed themselves to be "public servants of the people," and everything they did was "to serve the people."

David and Emily remembered that there were such kinds of people and such ugly monsters on Earth and that some ugly species would inevitably breed among living things. It was like flies and cockroaches mingling in the ranks of insects, also like viruses mixing with microorganisms.

Mr. Hallef said that such people were not only ugly but also evil, because they were actually such scums as bandits and hooligans in society.

They spread their fallacies and heresies, inciting the people to rebel and overthrow the legal regime, letting the people act as cannon fodders and form an army to fight for them. In the civil war, the compatriots killed each other, and these monsters only wanted to win power, and they took the opportunity to seize power.

David and Emily were a little surprised. Could it be that the heresy on Earth spread to other planets or even other universes?

"That's not surprising," said Ms. Merlin, "as long as there is the right climate, germs and viruses will breed, and just as ugly, just as vicious. That is, the crows in the world are generally black."

These demons claimed to rob the rich and assist the poor, but in fact, they robbed the rich and took their properties. After they seized power, they became new dignitaries.

They treated the people as mere slaves, draining the very life from them, sucking their bones and marrow. These demons and their descendants had held power for generations, tightening their grip and squeezing the people dry, one generation after another. They treated the country as their private property. They bent the law for selfish ends, corrupted, and many of them became billionaires. These monsters were full of fat, like round aphids with bulging bellies. They were aware of their sins and were worried about the safety of the huge amount of wealth illegally obtained. They deposited their wealth in foreign banks in case of liquidation by the domestic people in the future.

This group of demons brainwashed the people, proclaiming themselves as the saviors of the nation, promising to bring happiness to the people. They spread lies, claiming that the citizens of the Five-Thorn Kingdom were the happiest people in the world and that they, the demons, were the ones who had made it all possible. They encouraged the people to "sneakily enjoy their happiness," masking the truth with false promises.

However, the reality was exactly the opposite of their propaganda. Most of the people in their country lived below the poverty line.

In order to block the eyes and ears of the people, these demons built a "separation wall" on the border with neighboring countries. Domestic people were not allowed to have any contact with foreigners. If anyone dared to cross the wall and escape, the Five-Thorn National Border Guard and the police could shoot them on the spot. Nevertheless, many people in the country intended to escape from the sea of suffering and risked climbing over the wall in pursuit of freedom and happiness. The number of victims of the wall crossing was countless, whose bodies were piled up near the wall. It was said that life in foreign countries was better than that in the Five-Thorn Kingdom.

To prevent the people of the country from knowing the truth abroad, the Five-Thorn Kingdom built a *firewall* to prevent foreign news from being introduced into the country and let the people know the situation abroad.

Therefore, the Five-Thorn Kingdom was also called the *"Wall Country."*

David and Emily originally hoped to seek beauty and paradise in foreign countries and foreign lands, but they saw ugliness and callousness similar to those on Earth.

David and Emily learned that there used to be several influential religions here with many believers.

However, those in power in the Five-Thorn Kingdom refused to open up freedom of belief. They classified all religions as "cults," wantonly demolishing churches and temples, and persecuting heretics. In fact, their own fallacy was the real cult.

Mr. Charge, Mr. Hallef, and Ms. Merlin, friends of David and Emily, were all persecuted for believing in "hereticism" and using circumvention software to obtain foreign information.

In view of the suffocating political atmosphere in the country, David and Emily decided not to stay here for a long time and decided to leave the place for a country with relatively loose politics. Unexpectedly, they were blocked by the officials here.

The officials of the Five-Thorn Kingdom believed that David and Emily had illegally entered the country under unknown identities and were suspected of being foreign spies. They were deprived of their legal status as tourists in the country and imprisoned, losing their personal freedom.

The amulet of David and Emily was confiscated to prevent them from escaping with it.

David and Emily became prisoners in the Five-Thorn Kingdom. At that time, it was winter in the country. The cell was unbearably cold, and the air was stale.

David and Emily compared themselves to birds in a cage, recalling those free-spirited birds on Berde Star. They flew together or alone. After flying for a while, they could either perch on trees, or on the water's edge, drink water on the shore, or look for food in the grass, without any restraint.

At this time, David and Emily really felt that once freedom was lost, they knew how precious it was.

King Miragy, his relatives, senior officials, and important ministers became the privileged class of the country. These social moths were all well-nourished, energetic, healthy, and long-lived, enjoying special food, water, and air, as well as the best medical equipment and services in the country.

The secret of their longevity was to transplant organs. When some organs of their body were aging or slightly ill, they even took organs from healthy people for organ transplantation, trading the lives of innocent healthy people for their own health and longevity. This extreme evil was outrageous.

During this period, the king sent people to communicate with David and Emily, saying that if they met the official conditions of the country, they could restore their personal freedom.

The official conditions of the Five-Thorn Kingdom were that David and Emily should use the Divine Watch to go to the palace of the neighboring country Hoolla Kingdom to steal the country's national treasure *"Diamond Crown"* and bring it back to the Five-Thorn Kingdom. When it was done, David and Emily would be free.

The diamond crown of Hoolla was inlaid with twelve top-grade diamonds, which were rare in the world. The owner of the crown would have the highest authority in the world. So, the Hoolla Kingdom was the global hegemony of Demon.

King Miragy of the Five-Thorn Kingdom had coveted this for a long time and wanted to replace the Hoolla Kingdom as the global hegemony.

David and Emily were eager to be free. In addition, they learned that Lagifu, the king of Hoolla, was also a tyrannical dictator. In order to gain freedom, they intended to try their luck.

In this way, the official of the Five-Thorn Kingdom should return their Divine Watch to them. David and Emily were loyal and promised not to escape during this period.

The two activated the Divine Watch and the Magic Spell and came to the court of Hoolla Kingdom. Afraid of being discovered, the two shrunk themselves down to a size smaller than the crickets. So, no one would notice them. They searched the palace and finally found a secret room. They got in through the gap under the door. They saw the sparkling diamond crown. The diamond crown was indeed exquisite, with 12 large pieces of beautiful diamonds glistening from time to time.

David and Emily were almost stunned. The diamond crown was worthy of being a rare treasure. With Sapphires, emeralds, gold, and silver glitter. It was a priceless, high-end, and extremely luxurious human treasure and fine art.

In the secret room of the king, they restored their original figures with the Divine Watch and packed the priceless diamond crown into a box.

David and Emily returned to the Five-Thorn Kingdom with the help of their artifacts. Miragy, the king of the Five-Thorn Kingdom was overjoyed when he saw the rare treasure diamond crown he had been dreaming for. He ordered the royal palace to hold a banquet to celebrate the success of David and Emily, who were awarded as royal ministers. David and Emily didn't pay much attention to this and declined them. They only hoped that the king could fulfill his original promise and restore their freedom.

However, when David and Emily returned to the country after their meritorious service, their Divine Watch was officially confiscated, saying that the diamond crown and the Divine Watch were important instruments of the country. David and Emily thought that in this way, they would still be unable to leave the Five-Thorn Kingdom.

David and Emily's friend Mr. Charge and others said, "The officials never keep their promises. David and Emily should not have listened to the official lies and stolen the diamond crown for them in the first place. Demons are demons. One should have no faith in them."

David and Emily recounted the performance of stealing the diamond crown for the monarch. They deeply realized and regretted that they could have taken that opportunity to escape and should not have lost the opportunity to regain their own freedom.

With the stolen diamond crown, the Five-Thorn Kingdom gained the upper hand on the Demon Star, claiming to be the master of the world.

Before long, a new force sprang up on the Demon Star. A country called Micalley emerged and developed rapidly. The State of Micalley was originally a small area. President Schlare, the enlightened head of state, attached great importance to education and the development of science and technology, he had taken a substantial lead in the fields of science, technology, and economy. The country's national strength had greatly increased, and Micalley had become a powerful country. The country had the most modern military and armed forces in the world and was invincible on the Demon Star.

Although the Five-Thorn Kingdom had a diamond crown, it was obviously lagging behind in terms of technology and economy. King Miragy indulged in his own authority all day long and did not pay much attention to education and production. As a result, this country lacked talent and technology and could not produce high-quality silver films. In modern technology, without the silver films that kept pace with the times, it was difficult to keep pace with the advanced countries.

Miragy, the king of the Five-Thorn Kingdom, was worried that the backwardness of the Kingdom he ruled in the field of science and technology would inevitably lead to the decline of national strength. However, it was not easy to produce qualified silver films in a short period of time. He thought it over and over again and felt that the only way was to send David and Emily to the State of Micalley to steal the silver films and the technology of making silver films. This could only be done by David and Emily with their artifact.

In this way, David and Emily were called into the palace again. King Miragy repeatedly apologized for his failure to fulfill his promise to them after they had gained the diamond crown in Hoolla for him. He said that he valued talents too much and was not willing to let them leave, asking them to understand. And he once again commended them for their achievements in successfully gaining the diamond crown and completing the sacred mission last time.

A sinister smile appeared on King Milagy's ugly face. Yet, another sacred mission was assigned to David and Emily. This was to go to the country of Micalley and try to obtain the technology of making silver films and some ready-made high-end silver films, just like the last time when they went to the country of Hoolla to obtain the diamond crown. When David and Emily heard that they were going to do that disgraceful thing again, they looked embarrassed and tried their best to push back.

However, King Miragy made a supplicative gesture, saying that David and Emily were now the heroes of the Five-Thorn Kingdom and should put the overall situation first and serve the country.

At this time, David and Emily had another plan in mind, so they agreed to the errand verbally.

The Divine Watch was given back to David and Emily. They went to the state of Micalley at the king's order. They saw that the country was full of vitality; not only were the technology and economy thriving, and people living a rich life, but there was also political enlightenment. They abolished the monarchy, and the state was run by leaders and parliamentarians elected by the people. David and Emily felt that it was like a country of democracy on Earth.

They were invited to the highest government of the country of Micalley and met the leader, President Schlare. The president was approachable and met them in a friendly atmosphere. When David and Emily explained their intentions, the President smiled. He said that he knew Mr. Miragy very well, and King Miragy was eager to acquire silver films and silver film technology only for his autocratic rule. If King Miragy could transform his state into a democratic one and benefit the people, he was willing to transfer the silver film technology. David and Emily asserted that King Miragy could not do it.

David and Emily made up their minds to stay in the state of Micalley this time and not return to the Five-Thorn Kingdom. They wanted to be residents of Micalley and live a free and happy life here. In this way, the two stayed in the State of Micalley. They were valued by the country and promoted to the Ministry of Education to make their own contributions to the country's culture and education.

Miragy, the king of the Five-Thorn Kingdom, was furious when he learned about it. If arrested and brought to justice, they would be sentenced to severe punishment.

David and Emily informed his friends Mr. Charge, Mr. Hallef, and Ms. Merlin in the Five-Thorn Kingdom through modern means of communication. They unanimously appreciated and supported the actions of David and Emily. David and Emily suggested that they try to escape from the Five-Thorn Kingdom and come to

Micalley state. Later, with the help of David and Emily, Mr. Hallef and Ms. Merlin came to Micalley State with their families.

Miragy, the King of the Five-Thorn Kingdom, increasingly felt that the existence of the Micalley State was the greatest threat to his regime. Dazed by his power, he brazenly launched a war of aggression against the country of Micalley, under the pretext that Micalley had hijacked his important ministers and a powerful artifact from the Five-Thorn Kingdom, thus justifying his attack on Micalley.

The land of Micalley was small, and the Kingdom of Five-Thorn, a big country, planned to defeat the country and Emily committed treason and defection at home. of Micalley with a blitzkrieg within three to five days and destroy it. After conquering the country of Micalley, he could also obtain the silver films and silver film technology there by the way.

Unexpectedly, under the leadership of the young President Schlare, the Micalley

State rose up against the enemy and dealt a head-on blow to the invaders. It shattered the dream of the invaders to annex and crush the country of Micalley.

David and Emily's friend, Mr. Charge, failed to escape to the country of Micalley recently. He was conscripted into the army and captured in a battle, becoming a POW of Micalley's army. He realized his wish to escape to the state of Micalley.

In this way, David and Emily reunited with several of their good friends in the state of Micalley.

Both Mr. Charge and Mr. Hallef, who came to the country of Micalley earlier, joined the anti-aggression war against the Five-Thorn Kingdom. They fought against the enemy bravely and made repeated military exploits.

The Five-Thorn Kingdom was at war with the Micalley country, and the situation was getting unfavorable to the Five-Thorn Kingdom. The State of Micalley had the upper hand in the manufacture and use of weapons with the most advanced silver film. The outdated weapons of the Five-Thorn Kingdom were completely destroyed, and the morale of the soldiers was low.

The Five-Thorn Kingdoms had been losing ground on the battlefield. It was still impossible to win the war that had dragged on for half a year.

In order to restore the defeated situation, the Five-Thorn Kingdom unexpectedly adopted unconventional weapons of mass destruction. It spread a large number of deadly "poisonous cockroaches" to the Micalley country, causing a severe plague, and countless innocent people were killed by the poisonous beetles. The spread of poisonous cockroaches was completely out of control. A large number of poisonous cockroaches not only wreaked havoc in the country of Micalley but also spread all over the world, including the country of Five-Thorn Kingdom. It was like opening Pandora's magic box and causing a great disaster.

The epidemic had devastated human lives at an extremely fast speed. The elderly and those with underlying diseases were the first to die of poisoning, followed by middle-aged and even young people.

The tyrant of the Five-Thorn Kingdom wanted to use poisonous cockroaches to endanger the whole world, but even the common people in his own country were infected and died.

For this great crime against humanity, the authorities of the Five-Thorn Kingdom should have apologized to the world. Instead, those demons refused to admit their monstrous sins and even shifted the blame onto other countries.

During the epidemic, David and some local scientists worked together to discuss and study effective anti-epidemic methods. His major was biotechnology, which was useful now.

David and his colleagues had cultivated a kind of bumblebee with a stinger on its tail that could kill poisonous cockroaches. This was to fight poison with poison. This kind of bumblebee did not attack people, but specially dealt with poisonous cockroaches, which was the best way to solve the disaster of poisonous cockroaches.

Emily published many articles in the media to expose the ugly face of the dictator of the Five-Thorn Kingdom and the evil activities of murdering the people.

Emily's call for justice aroused the consciousness of people all over the world. People had a deeper understanding of the dangers of dictators to the country and society, so as to fight for democracy and freedom.

The Five-Thorn Kingdom was completely defeated, and the army of the Micalley State invaded the territory of the Five-Thorn Kingdom. Miragy, king of the Five-Thorn Kingdom, absconded in fear of crime. He fled to the Hoolla Kingdom and sought asylum in the Hoolla Kingdom on the condition of returning the diamond crown. The Hoolla Kingdom temporarily accepted him. The two tyrants means were like-minded and walked together like two miserable brothers.

Later, the insightful and oppressed people of Hoolla Kingdom rose up against the tyranny and overthrew Lagifu, the king of Hoolla, who had become a prisoner.

President Schlare of Micalley State urgently summoned David and Emily, asking them to go to the Kingdom of Hoolla immediately to capture the sinful lone thief Miragy with the help of the Divine Watch.

David and Emily did as they were told. Without further do, the two rushed to Hoolla Kingdom at once. Miragy, the king of the Five-Thorn Kingdom, lost his backer and hid everywhere alone.

When David and Emily arrived in the Kingdom of Hoolla, with the assistance of the local army, they caught the distraught Miragy in a hole in the ground.

At this time, King Milagy of the Five-Thorn Kingdom and Lagifu, the king of the Hoolla Kingdom, had been detained by the local army.

When King Miragy saw David and Emily, he begged them to spare his life for the sake of their old friendship.

David: Talking about old friendship, we will never forget the bitter days of being imprisoned by you in the Five-Thorn Kingdom. We can't forget the country of Micalley once" that was ravaged by your army, and the thousands of men, women, and children who were poisoned to death by your poisonous beetles.

Emily: Come on, Miragy. The trial of the International Court of Justice is waiting for you.

In desperation, Miragy had no choice but to get into the prison van, walking alongside David and Emily, heading directly to the International Court of Justice in Micalley.

After the prison van arrived at the capital of Micalley, it was discovered that Miragy had died in the prison van.

After inspection, he was found to have swallowed a poisonous cockroach in the car and died of poisoning.

Miragy, King of the Five-Thorn Kingdom, was well aware of his heinous crimes and could not escape the punishment of the law. His end must be hanged. So, he chose to take his own life.

At this time, the evil and ugly faces of the two dictators were completely exposed in broad daylight. Their painted skins were peeled off, and people recognized that they were genuine monsters. They had ferocious faces, red hair, and green faces, fierce and murderous, killing people without blinking an eye. It was said that Lagifu, King of the Hoolla Kingdom, after being arrested, became anxious and died of a sudden illness. After his death, he still wore the regained diamond crown.

The citizens of the Hoolla Kingdom believed that this dictator was not qualified to own the diamond crown and rule the world. The crown should be worn by a more fitting head of state, and that President Schlare of the State of Micalley deserved it.

Chapter 9

THE FOOL WORLD

avid and Emily came to the country Chiko on the planet Fulle by choosing on the Divine Watch.

The Divine Watch showed that this was a strange country. David and Emily came here with a special curiosity to experience what it was like to live in this strange country. The galaxy where Fulle star was located was the Red Sun System. In this system, there was a luminous and hot star similar to the sun, that was the "Red Sun."

The Red Sun Galaxy was much larger than the solar system, and the Golden Way System that contained the Red Sun Galaxy was times larger than the Milky Way.

The Red Sun constantly supplied light and heat to the planets in the galaxy. Light and heat were essential for human beings and all kinds of various creatures on the planet.

At this time, the world was already a modern society similar to that on Earth.

However, Piego, the head of the Chiko Empire, went against the trend of history and dreamed of being the emperor in the feudal society.

Piego believed himself to be the real Dragon Emperor, just like the Chinese emperors of all dynasties. He believed that his imperial power was bestowed by God. In fact, his power was granted privately by several gang bosses after careful negotiation. State power was the lifeblood of this gang. Democratic elections must never be implemented. Only by exercising totalitarian dictatorship could the regime of the mafia be guaranteed for thousands of years and never change color.

David and Emily noticed that the image of the dragon in the Chinese mind actually appeared on a planet in another universe, which was also the idol worshiped by common people in imperial society. In fact, the dragon is a non-existent species. It only exists in people's imagination. Its horns are like those of a deer, its head is like a camel, its claws are like an eagle, and its palms are like a tiger. It is a monster made up of the images of several animals.

Piego liked to sit on a chair inlaid with dragon shapes, which was the *dragon chair* that emperors of all dynasties sat on. When he sat on the resplendent dragon chair, he imagined that his subjects would shout "*Long live*" to him, and the pleasure of the emperor's dream would soar into the sky. He suddenly felt blissful, and as if he had become a real dragon cruising happily in the sky.

In fact, Piego had no inkling, no virtue, no talent, and his brain was full of paste and bad water. He was a complete bad guy. This person had only a primary school education, and his speeches were all written by his secretary. When reading the manuscripts, he often made mistakes in pronunciation, becoming the laughingstock of people.

When it came to modern thought and ideas of democracy, Piego was out of tune. And he always liked to boast complacently about the high efficiency of his totalitarian system.

The bosses of the black gang just took a fancy to him, so they entrusted him with an important responsibility.

Once, David and Emily talked about the Chiko Empire they were currently in.

David: As a majestic country, how can the Empire of Chiko tolerate such a foolish monarch?

Emily: I think that the Chiko Empire's regime is maintained by first relying on high pressure, and second by fooling the people. The army of the Chiko was mainly used to suppress the domestic people.

The Chiko Empire was brainwashing the people ideologically and forcing them to learn Piego's thoughts.

David: So, this country of Chiko we are in is a country of fools?

Emily: I don't think so. There are always clear-minded people, and there are plenty of them.

David: It is particularly important for a country to appoint the right leader.

Emily: That's the biggest difference between democracy and centralization.

David: The emperor in front of us is not virtuous and talented, but he can hold a high position. This country is bound to be destroyed by him.

Emily: Let's wait and see.

Piego had no political foresight. Whatever he did, big or small, failed. Piego had an idea only on a whim, patted his fat head, and made an important decision. This was known as "slapping the head decision." None of the decisions made in this way did not lead to incomplete projects.

Piego was skilled in power, but incapable of governing the country. He was overconfident and considered himself as the leader of a big country and of the world. He liked to point out the direction for the country and for the world at every turn.

He spread coins to the rulers of some poor countries in order to buy people's hearts internationally and win the support of these countries for him.

Piego was a stubborn, stupid mediocrity. No matter his appearance or work style, he looked like a stupid pig. So people secretly nicknamed him *"Pig."* When someone mentioned pig, others naturally associated it with him.

When Piego learned of this, he was furious and ordered to arrest anyone who dared to call him a pig. Not only that, he also ordered that the word "pig" be deleted in the language of the Chiko Empire. All dictionaries should exclude all entries with the word "pig." The word "pig" should be removed from all textbooks and important documents. It was like the ancient Chinese emperor who banned the same characters as those that appeared in his name. This was called a *"taboo word."*

As a result, some commonly used terms in daily life had to be changed. For example, "pork" was changed to "fat animal meat," "bristle" was changed to "fat animal" and so on, causing a lot of inconvenience to the people.

When Towa, a neighbor child, talked to his mother, who advised him to eat more food, he accidentally let slip the word "pig". He said, "I don't want to get fat, like a fat pig." The mother quickly covered his mouth with her hand to prevent the child from uttering the word *pig* and being heard by others. That would spell disaster for the child and the whole family.

At home, Piego's policies had lost all popular support, relying only on the flattery of his sycophants.

He was surrounded only by sycophants. Anyone with a clearer perspective or a more straightforward approach had either been pushed aside or cast out as troublemakers.

The sycophants blew trumpets for the emperor. The tone of the trumpet was blowing higher and higher, and the emperor was praised beyond belief.

Another superb flatterer and drummer put forward a surprising statement to the crowd. He said that Piego was like the Red Sun, and he was even brighter than the Red Sun. Under the unrestricted praise of the flatterers, Piego also thought that he was the Red Sun, and even had surpassed the Red Sun.

The sycophants said that the Red Sun rose when the emperor woke up in the morning and set when the emperor slept at night.

David and Emily experienced first-hand how absurd the country of fools could be. The operation of the Red Sun actually had to obey the orders of some small animal on a small planet. In comparison, the Red Sun with Emperor Chiko, this little animal was just a drop in the ocean.

David and Emily said that in that case, the operation of the galaxy in the entire universe would be changed. The Red Sun became Piego's entourage. One day when Piego slept late and hadn't woken up until noon, the Red Sun had to wait for Piego to open his eyes before slowly getting up.

Then that day should start late. One day when Piego was drinking wine and playing cards, he went to bed at midnight. The Red Sun had to wait for Piego to close his eyes before setting.

David and Emily's jokes were reported by some informants. When the emperor heard that someone dared to disrespect him, he flew into a rage and charged David and Emily, saying that they were guilty of the crime of illegally discussing government affairs and attempting to subvert the empire's power. David and Emily were then given a serious warning.

Piego's sycophants forced the subjects to dance the "Loyalty Dance" every day to express their infinite loyalty to the emperor. Someone revealed that David and Emily were not devoted enough and had a playful smile when they were dancing the Loyalty Dance. This disrespectful attitude towards the emperor aggravated their crimes.

Among Piego's sycophants, some masters put forward the theory that Piego was a "dragon species," or "the descendant of the dragon," and claimed that they had solid evidence to prove it.

A consummate sycophant and drummer presented an astonishing piece of *evidence* to the public.

He said that there were marks of dragon tail on Piego's buttocks. That trace could only be seen by people who were infinitely loyal to Piego. People who couldn't see the dragon tail on Piego's buttocks were those who were not loyal enough to Piego.

In this way, the citizens of the Chiko Empire rushed to the capital to watch Piego's ass. Piego also wanted to take this opportunity to test the loyalty of every citizen to him. Tens of thousands of people came to the capital to support the Emperor.

Piego met them smugly. The Emperor of Chiko stood on a tall platform, with his butt exposed to the public.

This reminded Emily of the Cultural Revolution in China in the middle of the 1960s when the Great Leader met fanatic young people from all over the country. They competed to express their love for the Great Leader.

All of the people present claimed to have seen traces of a dragon's tail on Piego's ass. Piego was ecstatic and convinced that he was the descendant of the dragon. He was the God-given king of the country.

Just as Piego arrogantly presented his butt to the entire nation, a sudden burst of bird droppings rained down from the sky, some of which landed squarely on his exposed backside. These bird feces were dirty and smelly, and everyone was dumbfounded for a while.

At this time, a talented sycophant expressed his brilliant insights. He said that the divine bird, the Phoenix, had just flown over the sacred gathering site and saw the descendant of the Dragon showing traces of the Dragon, so it rained auspicious rain and dew from the sky to congratulate the emperor.

Even so, Piego's entourage hurriedly wiped the emperor's buttocks, put on his pants, and ended the ceremony in a hurry.

David and Emily told the citizens of Chiko the following facts.

The dragon was not a real creature, but rather a construct—an image of a four-dimensional being, artificially assembled. As a totem of loyalty to the emperor, it served as a tool for the ruler to command respect and devotion from his subjects.

David and Emily also said that the closest animal to the dragon was the dinosaur. They had seen dinosaurs and lived with them for a period of time. Although dinosaurs were big, they were not sacred. They ate, drank, shat, peed, slept, mated, laid eggs, and raised children. They usually had a mild temper, but when fighting, they were extremely ferocious.

Some people said that the dragon was fake, but the dinosaur was real.

Others questioned the fact that David and Emily lived with dinosaurs for some time.

David and Emily told them that they used the Divine Watch to travel to the Dasor Star, where dinosaurs lived hundreds of millions of years ago, to experience the life of dinosaurs. They told some interesting stories about dinosaurs, such as their good friend Amanda and group leader Peter, and they turned into fossils in the same place hundreds of millions of years later. Everyone listened with gusto. They thought that dinosaur was more believable and authentic than the imaginary dragon.

In the country, Piego thought that his imperial power was boundless, and he treated the people as small people and fart people. He could oppress and persecute them wantonly, and he could cover the sky with one hand, but no one dared to speak out.

David and Emily decided to go to Piego and expose the dictator's lies face to face, so that the truth would be revealed to the world.

They should also go to Emperor Piego and directly expose his crimes, so as to make his crimes known to the world.

So, David set the Divine Watch to the palace where the emperor stayed, and Emily chanted the Magic Spell. The two suddenly appeared in front of Emperor Piego. The emperor turned pale with fright and was speechless for a while.

Piego: Y… Y…, You two, what are you doing here today when you trespassed on a royal property? Come on guys! Catch these two gangsters!

Emily: Your Majesty don't worry! Your guards have been locked up by us. They can't save you.

Piego: Are you going to rebel?

David: We're going to chat with you today.

Piego: Chat with me? One or two small people, fart people. Don't overestimate yourselves.

Emily: David, get tall. Let the emperor see.

David and Emily suddenly grew taller and taller, so that they broke through the roof of the palace, and finally became two giants as tall as the flagpoles. Under the giant's feet, Piego looked like a little mouse. He raised his head and looked up and stared at them dumbfounded. When he realized his situation, he felt panic and trembling all over.

David: Piego, look, are we still small people, fart people?

Piego: No! No! Forgive my short-sightedness. Please forgive me for offending you two.

Emily: Don't worry, Piego. We did not come to the palace this time to ask for your throne and your life although we can trample you to death as soon as we lift our feet. Believe it or not?

Piego: I believe it, I believe it. Now I am but an ant under your feet.

David: Do you think you are really a "descendant of the dragon?"

Piego: All the citizens saw the dragon tail on my butt.

Emily: In fact, all the citizens are lying to you.

There is no trace of a dragon's tail on your ass at all.

Piego: Is everyone lying to me?

David: Yes, that's right. Because anyone who tells the truth will be persecuted.

Emily: You made everyone lie.

Piego: Oh my God!

Emily: God's not on your side.

David: We just want you to know the truth. Don't oppress the people under your administration too much. Otherwise, they would all be giants like what we are today.

Emily: At that point, it's too late for you to regret it.

Piego: I know, I know.

David: We will spare your life today. But there is a condition.

Piego: Go ahead. I will do as long as I can.

David: The two of us are visitors from afar. We happened to pass by this place. We have noticed that your country's politics is too dark and fierce, the people are living in poverty, and the country is ruined. We can no longer tolerate this, so we've come to speak with you, to make you understand one truth: do not oppress the people too much.

Emily: If you go too far, your end will be very ugly.

Piego: I know, I know.

David: Don't think you are any kind of dragon. It's just a fool's dream.

Emily: You have no talent or virtue, just a fool.

Piego: Yes, yes.

For the convenience of speaking, David and Emily changed back to their original figures. Seeing the stretching and shrinking of these two people, Piego was stunned.

David: Today is a modern society. Democracy and freedom are a powerful trend in the world. The autocratic system of the imperial power of the Chiko State should be thrown into the garbage heap of history.

Emily: You stupid and incompetent should have given up the imperial power long ago and let more intelligent and wiser people here lead the country.

Pigeon: Oh, My God! What kind of system would that be? A country cannot live without an emperor. I will be responsible for my subjects to the end.

David: If you step down, it will be a great fortune for the country and the people.

Emily: Your people will forgive you.

Piego: It matters a lot. Let me think about it.

David: We're going to leave this planet soon and go to another planet. After we're gone, I hope you'll take care and behave yourself.

Piego: The two of you turned out to be knights from afar, respectable.

Emily: See you later.

Piego: See you later.

David: I hope the situation here will improve when we come next time.

Piego: Certainly, certainly.

Chapter 10

THE INTELLIGENT WORLD

avid and Emily came to a country called Veilty on the star of Wiss through their choice of the Divine Watch.

The country was politically enlightened, with a high degree of cultural education and human civilization, which exceeded the level of the most developed countries on the planet.

There is a sky beyond the sky, and there are people beyond people. It seemed that the wisdom of the people of Veilty state on the Wiss star was no less than that of the people on Earth.

The people here enjoyed full freedom of belief. Several major religions had large numbers of believers. The city was dotted with churches and temples. Although different religions believed in different Gods, they all believed in the omnipotence of Heaven and respected the will of God. Of course, there were atheists and unbelievers here too. In recent years, there was a vanguard force in the political and technological elite circle here. Based on the current rapid development of technology, they put forward the theory that AI technology would rejuvenate the country and AI would transform the world. This force had a tendency to be anti-traditional and deviation from God.

The opposite of this trend of thought was the traditional, God-worshiping conservative forces.

David and Emily were quite congenial to the common people here in the concept of worshipping Heaven.

The power of rejuvenating the nation through science and technology spread rapidly, leading to significant technological advancements and establishing the country as a leader in innovation.

At the same time, human wisdom had been exaggerated, and the role and power of God had been squeezed. The arrogance of human intelligence was rampant. There was a tendency to push God down from the altar and let the human elites control the whole universe. What was more, some people had proposed to let AI's new technology elites show off as a single flower, and the rest of mankind would be eliminated and become the garbage of history.

As soon as they set foot on the territory of the country, David and Emily felt that the automation and artificial intelligence here had taken an overwhelming advantage in all aspects of life. Their original living habits and working styles had to be adjusted and adapted.

The service and manufacturing industries here had largely been replaced by robots. In most cases, one had to deal with robots. Although these robots worked skillfully, rarely made mistakes, and had a serious and thoughtful attitude, David and Emily still felt a sense of loss. They were more accustomed to interacting with real people than to placing themselves in the jungle of robots woven of plastic, metal, and circuit boards. In comparison, they felt more natural and cheerful being in the wilderness among the fauna.

AI technology had flourished in this country for a while and was constantly upgrading, especially when the software designed with AI technology won the world championship in the chess competition. AI technology was widely used in various fields of human beings, and its accuracy and speed exceeded that of human beings. When AI technology replaced human beings in terms of design and planning ability, those AI enthusiasts were even more dazed by the victory and proposed that AI was crushing human intelligence. It was also said that the human brain was an old machine, which should be replaced with a constantly updated AI.

They even put forward the notion that AI would become a powerful force independent of the human brain, using AI to design and transform everything of human beings, thus destroying existing human beings in one stroke. So, they proposed that the end of modern mankind had arrived.

They believed that the products designed and manufactured by AI were superior to human products, and the development plan formulated by AI was superior to human planning. Therefore, humans should gradually give way to AI, accept their defeat, and hand over the future of mankind to AI.

David and Emily always had reservations about this notion.

They believed that AI was created and designed by humans. Although its ability could surpass human beings in many aspects, it would never surpass human beings in a deeper level of originality and imagination. It was like God who created people and everything in the world and in the universe, while AI would never be able to do it. AI's ability was far from being comparable to that of God. It could not replace Heaven, nor could it replace the entire human race.

The avid pursuers of AI in the country of Veilty had designed a plan to use the power of AI to teach David and Emily, the two conservatives from outer space, a lesson.

They took Emily to another city and placed the AI Emily they designed and controlled beside David. This AI Emily was not only identical to the real Emily in appearance but also exactly the same in personality and behavior as the real Emily.

In terms of perfection, it even surpassed the real Emily.

The designers of AI Emily had high expectations for their product, thinking David would accept this new Emily without reservation and forget about the old Emily.

At the same time, they placed an AI David beside Emily. This AI David was not only the same as the real David in appearance, but also in personality and behavior.

In terms of perfection, it even surpassed the real David.

Likewise, AI designers had high expectations for their product, thinking that Emily would accept the new David without reservation and forget the old David.

Unfortunately, the expectations of these AI pursuers failed.

For AI Emily, David was initially quite accommodating. It was quite normal to live and eat together with AI Emily every day, greeting each other, saying hello, and all in tune. However, once it came to emotions deep in her heart, AI Emily appeared very indifferent. The deep love, communication, and fusion that permeated the soul were all missed. David increasingly felt that this AI Emily resembled the robot Wilda Wika he had encountered at the Beauty Garden in Wonderland, yet the difference between them was as vast as a thousand miles, far from the essence of the real Emily.

For AI Emily, David was extremely indifferent, and the two were in the same room, but they were strangers. David missed Emily every day who was forced to separate from him. He even felt that he couldn't leave Emily for a while. He disdained the AI Emily in front of him.

Similarly, Emily was initially tolerant of AI David. As time went on, she felt that there was something wrong between the two of them. The relationship, emotion, and mutual communication and coordination between Emily and AI David could only stay at a superficial level and could no longer go deep. The too shared a room, but they were strangers. In Emily's eyes, AI David was just a decently made robot. Emily missed David who was forced to separate from her every day. She even felt that she couldn't live without David for a moment. She disdained the AI David in front of her.

After a period of time, under the strong protest and demand of David and Emily, AI suitors reluctantly withdrew AI David and AI Emily from their sides, and reluctantly admitted the failure of their plan. David and Emily reunited after a long separation, and they cherished their common feelings and life even more.

AI pursuers were not reconciled to the failure of their first plan to transform David and Emily. They deliberately included David and Emily in their second plan. This was to let David and Emily live in a zone without people. In this area, everyone David and Emily encountered were not real people, but AI beings—advanced robots, created to mimic human life.

David and Emily must deal with people in their lives, such as shopping, negotiating, requesting services, seeing a doctor, paying bills, etc. Pedestrians on the road, passengers on the bus, and service staff in all walks of life were all AI people.

The AI robots' dull faces, monotonous language, forced smiles, and mechanical gestures were tiresome. David and Emily even felt that they were being tortured now.

At this time, they really missed the feeling of interacting with real people and even animals. They had been on several uninhabited planets. Now, they would rather see the wilderness or primitive forest in front of them and all kinds of living animals, rather than the high-end machinery, fake faces, fake words, fake expressions and so on.

David and Emily were bored at the moment. They raised their voices and shouted loudly, sang to their heart's content. They even danced on the ground, imitating the movements of the robots, their arms moved rhythmically and swung left and right, and their legs moved rhythmically and stepped forward. They laughed and laughed to relieve their boredom.

David: AI is the fruit of human wisdom. Excessive use of it will cause today's situation.

Emily: AI chess software, and AI navigation GPS are widely used, the Internet has entered every aspect of people's lives, and robot technology has made rapid progress. All these achievements have provided great convenience to human beings in a short time. This made some people hot-headed, and there was fanatical worship and superstition of AI, and even the absurd prediction that AI people would eliminate human beings.

David: But all these high-tech achievements have their limitations. While AI chess software and AI navigation GPS may contain vast amounts of data and possess remarkable processing speed, they still fall short when compared to human intelligence in many other areas. However, once it involves the deeper layers of human emotions and psychology, and touches the depths of the human soul, AI will appear powerless. The mathematical models on which AI technology relies are clumsy in some areas.

Emily: Someone tried to use AI technology to engage in artistic creation, using data analysis and synthesis to create paintings, music compositions, dramas, and films. In terms of detail processing and personal style, AI technology replaces the artist himself. It can be seamless, to the point of confusing the real.

David: In that case, art can be mass production.

An art factory or workshop can replace an artist.

Emily: I don't like such "artistic products."

Actually, they cannot be regarded as art. Such products have completely lost the qualification and value of art.

David: Artists and works of art are bound to depreciate greatly.

Emily: Actually, not everything in the world can be digitized. The world created by God is much more complex than what people can understand and control. In fact, people's cognition of all things in the world is still quite superficial.

David: If you think that God creates and controls the world in a digital mode, and programs the future of human beings, it is really ignorant. Humans overestimate themselves and underestimate the omnipotence of God.

Emily: AI cultists are somewhat unrealistic.

David: Human beings are created by the Heavens and cannot be destroyed by human power.

David and Emily came up with a game to amuse themselves with AI under the situation of boredom.

They added some programs to a male robot and a female robot respectively, allowing them to be in a love affair. The male robot is called Daniel, and the female robot is called Jessica. The two started chatting.

Daniel: May I invite you to dinner tonight?

Jessica: OK.

Danicl: After dinner, let's go to see a movie together, shall we?

Jessica: Okay. In fact, I have long known about these old ways of hooking up with women.

After dinner and watching the movie, they chatted together again.

Daniel: Jessica, I love you.

Jessica: Daniel, you want me to say that I love you too, right?

Daniel: Jessica, honestly, do you love me too?

Jessica: Don't talk nonsense. What do machines like us love or not?

Daniel: Although I am not a real person, I can see that you are so beautiful, so gentle and so lively. How can I not love you? Otherwise, wouldn't I be heartless?

Jessica: Your chest is filled with a few circuit boards and chips. I'm tired of hearing such sweet talk tricks. Stop putting on airs.

Daniel: I am an advanced and upgraded version of AI. I have human feelings. I have children and carry on the family line through generations.

Jessica: Quit your nonsense. Do you and I have any fertility function?

Daniel: Possibly. If I sleep with you, I will make you pregnant.

Jessica: Daniel, stop bragging. How can I get pregnant when God doesn't assign me any DNA?

Daniel: Oh, that's true. You are right. No matter how smart we robots are, we don't have our own souls, nor the DNA endowed by God.

Jessica: Well, it's time to end our little farce. David and Emily laughed heartily.

David and Emily felt suffocated in the uninhabited arca of the country, which was beyond their endurance.

Therefore, they used their Divine Watch to escape from that area.

David and Emily came to a place where real people and AI people lived together. Here they could get in touch with some real people and feel more comfortable, because after all, there was still a little "popularity" here.

The AI pursuers were surprised to find that David and Emily escaped from the uninhabited area to the mixed area because the two areas had been blocked by AI technology. The people who were blocked in the no-man zone were almost unable to escape.

Under people's hard questioning, David and Emily had no choice but to reveal the mystery of their possession of the Divine Watch and said that this watch was a gift from Heaven.

This matter had made headlines in the country of Veilty. The divine power of the Divine Watch far exceeded the country's leading AI technology. Knowing that David and Emily came here from the original universe and planet with the Divine Watch the avid admirers of AI in the country of Veilty were even more shocked. They had once believed their AI technology was far ahead of all mankind, never anticipating that something unexpected would emerge along the way, leaving them puzzled.

AI fanatics in the country of Veilty proposed that David and Emily transferred the Divine Watch technology, and promised to give them generous remuneration.

David and Emily said that the Divine Watch was a gift from Heaven, and they did not master its design principles, let alone the patent rights.

After discussion, these people planned to let David and Emily display the Divine Watch in the downtown square, claiming to do some research on the structure and function of the amulet. They invited the top AI technologists from Veilty state, and a large number of citizens came to watch and witness the miracle.

David and Emily stayed at home these days, surrounded by AI people and things, and felt very depressed. Now it was a good opportunity to show up and perform in public. Why not?

When David and Emily came to the scene, they saw a sea of people in the square, and the jury composed of AI technology elites was sitting on the rostrum.

David and Emily first performed "Instant Crossing."

They announced that they would appear on the top of the 20-story building opposite the square in a flash David turned the Watch to the marked position, and Emily chanted the Spell. Almost at the same time, David and Emily appeared on the top of the tall building opposite the square. There was a lot of applause and cheers.

David and Emily easily returned to the square from the roof in the same way.

At the request of the audience, David and Emily performed their *magic talent* of shrinking and growing in size. Amidst the amazed eyes and cheers of admiration, people saw that these two people became the size of small rabbits for one moment, and giants for another. People couldn't believe their eyes, feeling like watching a superb trick, and opened their mouths wide involuntarily.

The members of the jury sitting on the rostrum and the national scientific and technological elites were embarrassed. Their claimed AI scientific and technological achievements and theories seemed to collapse in an instant. In the face of these facts, they suddenly became pale and powerless. At least those technological giants could not explain today's miracle. The AI power that claimed to be able to eliminate human beings seemed to be vulnerable.

After the grand performance in the square, the technology giants of the country invited David and Emily to the National Academy of Sciences to discuss the issue of the artifact.

In the discussion with David and Emily, the biggest difference among the technology giants was the question of "man conquers Heaven" or "Heaven conquers man."

AI technology giants still adhered to the principle of "man can conquer Heaven," unable to accept the concept of "God wins over man."

David and Emily cited the fact that the Divine Watch was "gifted from God". AI technology giants required that the Divine Watch to be submitted to them for in-depth study before making a final conclusion.

In order to discern the truth, David and Emily agreed to lend the watch to AI technology giants for five days. David and Emily would demonstrate the use of the Divine Watch and the Magic Spell, let them carefully examine and study it, and then announce the research results and conclusions to the whole country and the world.

Three days later, the results came out. Through the examination of the internal structure and basic functions of the Divine Watch, it became clear that this device surpassed the limits of both human and AI design and control. Notably, its activation depended on an external signal—the Magic Spell. This was beyond the limits of human intelligence. So, this was a *"divine artifact"*, not an AI product.

After the news was released to the world, it caused an uproar all over the world. AI's omnipotent myth declared bankruptcy.

Two senior leaders of the Veilty National Academy of Sciences committed suicide, taking responsibility and apologizing for their scientific and technological mistakes and misleading the public with their precious lives.

David and Emily were deeply moved by the responsible spirit of these two senior leaders. Hearing that the two senior leaders died after taking a deadly poison, David and Emily asked the local doctor if there was any way to save them. They were told that there was a resurrection water that the dead could be brought back to life in a short time. But that kind of water could only be collected on a small island called Divine Spring Island, thousands of miles away. It was impossible to go to the island to fetch water in a short time. David and Emily made a prompt decision, and with the help of the Divine Watch, they rushed to the Island immediately, brought back the resurrection water, and rescued the two senior leaders. This incident became a good story in the local area.

David and Emily decided to leave the country of Veilty and travel to the neighboring nation of Walto for a tour and investigation. They had heard that Walto was a remarkable place, home to a group of extraordinary people known as the Wattos.

Although the Walto people were in a new era of civilization and progress, their lives were deliberately distant from modern society, new technology, and new ideas.

They did not use electricity, gas, or cars, nor did they use radios, televisions, and the Internet.

They used kerosene lamps for lighting at night and firewood for heating in winter.

They advocated a natural and organic way of life.

They advocated humility and disliked pride.

They valued religious freedom and believed in God, willing to submit to God's will.

David and Emily appreciated the Walto people's way of life and philosophy. They just felt that modern human civilization should not be completely rejected. To those AI zealots in Veilty, the natural followers of

Walto seemed to be at the other end of the spectrum.

David and Emily were able to adjust to the simple and unpretentious life there during their stay in the country of Walto, because they did not pursue luxury and had more similar experiences when living with animals. They just felt that in the world of modern people, there was no electricity, no modern communication, and no network, which was a great defect and inconvenience.

David and Emily persuaded these people to properly accept some modern technologies and concepts. This was beneficial and harmless to them and their descendants. If they blindly isolated themselves from the modern world, they would become an outmoded group of mankind.

It was difficult for the Waltos to change their habits of generations. The Walto people were still willing to repeat the way of life of their ancestors.

In the autumn of that year, the country of Walto unfortunately suffered a major disaster. The violent storm lasted for more than ten days, and floods and tsunamis submerged a large number of residential houses.

At this critical juncture, David and Emily immediately activated the Divine Watch and went to the neighboring country of Veilty to ask for help. A large number of ships and helicopters were sent to the country of Walto to rescue people, and most of the affected people survived. There were many small AI helicopters in the rescue team as the main force, and the efficiency was extremely high.

After the disaster, the people of Walto thanked God for this and also thanked the people of Veilty who were technologically advanced. They were more aware of the importance of advanced technology. If it was not for the immediate rescue of the Veilty people with advanced technology, the country of Walto would have been in danger of annihilation and genocide.

David and Emily had traveled to ten planets in outer space so far. Whether they were on uninhabited or inhabited planets, they had gained a lot of insight, understood a lot of principles of the world and life, deepened their understanding of some issues, and even had a new understanding of some issues.

Chapter 11

THE PERFECT WORLD

avid and Emily found a planet on the display of the Divine Watch. It was called Perfee.

According to the information provided by the Divine Watch, it was a nearly perfect world, a world that everyone yearned for. Just having the chance to go there and take a look was considered a stroke of luck.

Without hesitation, David and Emily got there by the power of the Divine Watch.

Their initial impression of this place was that it was a bigger and more wonderful planet than the Earth. It was colorful, and also more exciting than the planets they visited in the past few years. As soon as they came to this *"Perfee Star"*, David and Emily were fascinated by everything there. There was no country ruled by a leader on this planet, and the whole human settlements were naturally integrated.

In this world, there was no government, no army, no prison, no police, no bank, and no currency.

Working here was a kind of happiness, and helping others was a kind of joy.

It was even better than the Wonderland David and Emily had been to eleven years ago.

The people here looked healthy and strong, their faces appeared happy and confidant. David blended in with the local crowd, making it hard to differentiate, because his height and image were quite similar to the local men. The Oriental image of Emily added another beautiful color to the crowd.

In addition to being warm and friendly, the people here were polite and gave people a sense of civilization.

David and Emily were amazed by this scene. Could all humans really be like this?

The relationships between humans on Earth had long been marked by divisions and conflicts. Disputes were constant, and the struggles seemed never-ending.

Human beings on this planet were full of harmony and friendship.

This level of harmony and friendship was simply extraordinary, unmatched by anything humans had experienced on any other planet. David and Emily came here, with a language barrier, and everything was strange to them. However, they did not feel any inconvenience.

The local people took the initiative to introduce everything here to them in an easy-to-understand way, and warmly and thoughtfully helped them arrange their accommodation, which was more friendly and considerate than the service staff of the seven-star hotels on Earth. And the consumption here was free.

They also told David and Emily which restaurants, cafes, parks, theaters, and sports venues were nearby.

In short, David and Emily were like distinguished guests and family members. The people here made them feel warm and comfortable, like at home.

The human life here was very different from that on Earth.

People lived in harmony with each other, and also with animals. Animals lived in harmony with each other.

Animal meat was completely excluded from human food.

It was replaced by more nutritious and tasteful food.

Meat was no longer part of restaurant menus, and fast-food chains that used to be meat-based had switched to non-meat ingredients. Chefs could create delicious meals without meat, far better than meat dishes on Earth.

The fast food here was more delicious. After eating a few times, David and Emily no longer recalled burgers and fried chicken, etc that they were used to. The carnivores of animals here, such as lions, tigers, leopards, and wolves, had changed into herbivores.

David and Emily saw this kind of animal eating grass and leaves as intently as sheep and deer.

They had witnessed black bears playing with jumping fish in the water without devouring them.

They saw the young lions sucking milk under the belly of the cow. The cow took the lion cub, as its children.

They witnessed the ferocious crocodile becoming amiable and eating plants and fruits on the shore. Frogs hopped around on their backs.

They saw the poisonous snake dance with the rabbit, and the wolf and the sheep sang together.

They witnessed anteaters stopped eating ants and atc grass seeds instead.

David and Emily were fascinated by everything about Perfee.

David: This is a perfect world. Everything we see here makes us happy.

Emily: Yes. Perfection in my mind includes the "truth, goodness, and beauty" pursued by human beings. "Truth, goodness, and beauty" has been fully realized here. It can bring me the greatest joy and happiness.

David: Falseness, evil, and ugliness are hard to hide here. Falsehood, lies, forgery, deceit, exaggeration, slander, etc. disappeared here. We no longer see the kind of mutual calculation, intrigue, self-interest at the expense of others, and even violent fights between people on the Earth. Disagreement among people is resolved through full discussion and friendly consultation.

Emily: I've never been so happy as I am here. I couldn't be happier!

David: It seems that the so-called paradise is not an unattainable realm, and the so-called Heaven is not an unattainable peak.

Emily: This is the paradise that people yearn for and pursue. Here is the beautiful Garden of Eden.

David and Emily had traveled to several planets. Neither the unmanned world nor the human world was as perfect as today's Perfee star.

Every day, David and Emily spent the best time of their lives in a relaxed and merry way.

David collected information on the Internet and did some research. He also kept a diary and wrote down every day and even every moment he spent here.

Emily used a room as a studio to describe various beautiful scenes here in her paintings. She felt that everything here was like a beautiful painting. She took photos of these paintings and planned to bring them back to the Earth for people to see.

David: I would spend the rest of my life here if it wasn't for missing my loved ones on Earth.

Emily: Our parents and children are probably thinking of us at this time too.

David: We are lucky to come to this perfect world and to experience the feeling of paradise, which is also the greatest happiness in our lives.

Emily: Yes. I think we should end this interstellar travel, return to the Earth, where we were apart for 6 years, and return to our home in Colorado. After all, we lived there for most of our lives. I miss our parents, our son, and our daughter so much.

David and Emily decided to end their extraordinary trip and return to Earth.

They bid farewell to the warm and friendly residents of Perfee Star and prepared to embark on the voyage home. A large number of residents of Perfee came out to see them off, wishing them a pleasant journey and inviting them to visit again in the future.

David and Emily told everyone that they had traveled to ten different planets before they visited here. In comparison, this Perfee star brought them the greatest satisfaction and happiness.

David and Emily shed tears of happiness, saying "Bye, bye!" to the persons seeing them off.

The two activated their Divine Watch and disappeared without a trace in an instant.

When David and Emily landed, they were surprised to find that they were not back home but were still at the original spot before they came to Perfee Star, that was, the Intelligent world of Wiss Star.

David checked the watch to see if there was anything wrong with it. He found that the name "Utopia" was clearly marked on the position of the perfect world of Perfee Star, which was determined on the Divine Watch by them last time. Their travel record of the Perfee Star on the Divine Watch was also blurred and turned into nothing.

David and Emily realized that their trip to Perfee was just a sleepwalking. The so-called perfect world of Perfee Star did not exist in this universe.

David and Emily's interstellar roaming lasted six years, traveling to ten planets and they had seen ten different worlds in the Big Sun and Red Sun Galaxies, Universe B. The ten planets were:

Dasor Star, the Dinosaur World

Inset Star, the Insect World
Janger Star, the Jungle World
Orson Star, the Water World
Berde Star, the Bird World
Humin Star, the Human World
Glute Star, the Gluttonous World
Demon Star, the Demon World
Fulle Star, the Fool World
Wiss Star, the Intelligent World

All these stars had been named by David and Emily, since nobody else except them had ever been there, and nobody else from the Earth had ever been to the Universe.

David and Emily's journey and adventures on ten planets, their trace and duration on each star were recorded in their Divine Watch.

Postscript

The Divine Artifact Inherited

2026 AD

Before they knew it, David and Emily had set foot on the ground of Boulder, Colorado, USA, the Earth, the Solar System, the Milky Way, Universe A. They spent almost no time traveling the distance of countless light years, which was still unbelievable for them. They had been away from their home and loved ones for six years, having traveled to several planets. Now, when they returned home, they could not help but feel a thousand emotions.

They had mixed feelings about being at home again. Looking at the old house, they felt very cordial. The old trees in the courtyard appeared older, and the bushes were sparse, all showing the passage of time. Lily, the cat at home, had begun to show signs of aging, walking slowly in the yard. However, she could still recognize her masters and took the initiative to approach David and Emily. Emily picked her up and stroked her hair. She made a grunt to express her happiness.

David and Emily left home six years ago to roam ten planets in universe B, and now they returned to their home on Earth in universe A.

It was a weekend afternoon. David's father and mother were naturally very happy to see their son and daughter-in-law who had been away from home for six years. When Oliver and Sophia saw their father and mother, being extremely excited, they ran forward and hugged them, looking at their parents' faces, and saying, "Dad, Mom, you are back. We missed you so much these years!"

David: Thank goodness we're finally back.

Emily: We missed you all the time outside. How have you been these years?

David's Mother: We're okay, We're okay. Your father was infected with COVID-19, but he recovered later.

Sophia: Our dog, Tommy is dead. We buried him in the backyard and set up a small tombstone for him.

David's mother: The life span of a dog is only ten years or more. Tommy had lived for 14 years, which is considered a long life.

David: It's not convenient for us to carry things with us when we come here, we only brought some dried alien fruits. We don't know what to call them. Try it, everyone.

Emily took out some chestnut-like nuts and put them on the table. Everyone tasted it, and the taste was particularly delicious and refreshing. Everyone was full of praise for this food from afar.

Emily: That's what we ate on uninhabited alien planets.

Sophia: Dad, Mom, what are aliens like? Tell us something about it, OK?

David: We'll tell you about those things later. We went to ten planets in another universe, some were uninhabited, and some were populated. Circumstances were so varied, and the stories were so twisted and strange that it would take many days for us to tell them to you in detail.

Sophia: Let's talk about "one thousand and one night" then.

David: OK, OK. We'll tell you stories in "One Thousand and One Night."

Emily: Those stories are better than the stories of One Thousand and One Night.

Oliver: Any adventure stories?

David: Of course. For many times, your mother and I narrowly escaped danger and death.

David's mother: Let's not talk about those things first. It's heartbreaking.

Oliver: Now I have grown up. I also want to travel and take risks like my parents.

Emily: My child, you have no magic artifact.

It's too unsafe outside.

Oliver: If we only think about safety, we will never be adventurers.

Sophia: I want to go on an adventure with my brother too.

Emily: All right, all right, let's talk about it later. David's mother: Dinner is ready. Let's eat together.

We haven't eaten together for years.

David and Emily felt very warm at home. But they often recalled the life on the extraterrestrial planets. And at the same time, they thought about various issues related to human beings, animals, and the universe and summarized their experiences and views on matters during their trip.

Emily had an old acquaintance, Mr. S, a Chinese-American who also lived in Colorado. Mr. S had a close relationship with David and Emily and was very familiar with their situation. He wrote and published the book "World's End and the Sea Angle" in 2020. The book vividly chronicled and interpreted the love and adventure of Emily and David, while also recounting his early experiences in China. It was said that some of Mr. S's own stories were the prototypes of the character Ye Qiuming in the book "World's End and the Sea Angle."

David and Emily's son Oliver and daughter Sophia loved the book *"World's End and the Sea Angle"* very much and admired their parents' courage and wisdom. They heard that Mr. S was now writing a book about their parents' recent expeditions to extraterrestrial places. The publication of this book was eagerly awaited.

The story of David and Emily traveling around ten stars in the outer universe with their Divine Watch and Magic Spell quickly spread throughout the country and the world. The two were repeatedly invited to give speeches and symposiums in relevant departments. They were also invited by their alma mater, University of Colorado at Boulder as visiting professors to teach in related majors. David mainly taught biology and cosmology, and Emily mainly taught fine art and philosophy.

At the same time, David and Emily fulfilled the requests of their son and daughter, sharing fascinating stories about the outer world and aliens with them every day. Oliver and Sophia listened eagerly, captivated by each tale.

In this way, after three years, about a little over a thousand and one days since their return home. David and Emily's storytelling to the children had been finished.

2029 AD

Some readers here may ask, the book "Interstellar Roaming" was released in 2023, how can it involve stories that happened in 2029, which is six years later? In the author's opinion, this matter is not surprising. Since the book explores, in one chapter, the age of dinosaurs from hundreds of millions of years ago, and in the author's other work, *World's End and the Sea Angle,* it portrays the future world a thousand years from now, the contrast between past and future is striking. In some specific space-time coordinates, it's not out of tune to talk about what will happen six years later here.

That year, Oliver was 22 years old and had finished college, Sophia was 17 and had finished high school.

At home, Oliver and Sophia were suddenly found missing. And the Divine Watch also disappeared, most probably because they took it away.

David and Emily were worried about this, and David's parents were even more anxious. They blamed David and Emily for telling their children those adventure stories.

David and Emily said that the children took the Divine Watch, but they had no Magic Spell and could not use it.

So, the Divine Watch could not protect them. According to David and Emily, when the children found the amulet useless, they would probably come back soon.

However, after a few days, the children did not come back. After many days, the children still did not come back. David and Emily speculated that one possibility was that the children still went on an adventure in the distance without the help of the Divine Watch and the Magic Spell. Another possibility was that God was moved by the courage of the two children and gave the Watch to Oliver and Sophia. Sophia got a new Magic Spell. David and Emily thought about it and assumed that the second possibility was more likely the case.

After many days, David and Emily found a letter left by the two children, which was almost the same as what David and Emily said in the letter before they left home six years ago.

Dear grandparents and parents,

We love each of you.
Please forgive us for leaving without saying goodbye to you. Please forgive us for our willful behavior this time.
The Almighty God met us in a dream. The renewed Divine Watch with the Magic Spell has been transferred to us as gifts.

We are grateful for it.

We are willing to complete the sacred mission entrusted to us by God with our modest strength.

We will strive to do a good job in this investigation.

Goodbye, grandparents and parents. We know that the journey is bound to be full of risks. It is also possible that we will never come back again. In that case, we will bid farewell forever to you at this moment. We sincerely thank our grandparents and parents for their upbringing and teaching……..

We have the blessing and protection of God, and the help of the artifact. We believe that everything will be as expected and look forward to our reunion in the future.

Oliver Polo and Sophia Polo

The next generation of David and Emily, Oliver and Sophia, inherited their parents' careers and were traveling around with the Divine Watch and Magic Spell.

There are countless mysteries in the universes waiting for people to explore.